Dear Reader

DIRTY WEEKEND is very special to me because, just like Caz Ryan, I recently moved from the town to the country. Fuelled by my experiences, Caz and Galem's story just flew, and even though it's very different from my usual style I couldn't resist sharing it with you. I was thrilled when this story found a home with Modern Extra!

Galem is very much an alpha male, and Caz is two girls in one, which keeps him guessing. I love these two characters, and they certainly sparked both my imagination and my humour.

What happens when a man goes searching for his roots and a woman tries to forget hers? The romantic village of Hawkshead provides the setting, and Galem Brent provides the answer.

I hope Caz and Galem find their way into your heart as they did into mine, and I hope you'll be looking out for my next Modern Extra, where I'll be turning the tables on a country girl and placing her smack bang in the centre of the city.

Happy reading, everyone.

Susan

PS And remember you can always contact me at susan@susanstephens.net

D1460320

Susan Stephens was a professional singer before meeting her husband on the tiny Mediterranean island of Malta. In true Modern™ style they met on Monday, became engaged on Friday, and were married three months after that. Almost thirty years and three children later, they are still in love. (Susan does not advise her children to return home one day with a similar story, as she may not take the news with the same fortitude as her own mother!)

Susan had written several non-fiction books when fate took a hand. At a charity costume ball there was an after-dinner auction. One of the lots, 'Spend a Day with an Author', had been donated by Mills & Boon® author Penny Jordan. Susan's husband bought this lot, and Penny was to become not just a great friend but a wonderful mentor, who encouraged Susan to write romance.

Susan loves her family, her pets, her friends and her writing. She enjoys entertaining, travel, and going to the theatre. She reads, cooks and plays the piano to relax, and can occasionally be found throwing herself off mountains on a pair of skis or galloping through the countryside. Visit Susan's website: www.susanstephens.net—she loves to hear from her readers all around the world!

*If you can't wait for Susan's next Modern Extra be sure to look out for her contribution to **The House of Niroli** in Modern Romance™ this November!*

Recent books by the same author:

Modern Romance™

ONE-NIGHT BABY
BEDDED BY THE DESERT KING
IN THE VENETIAN'S BED

DIRTY WEEKEND

BY
SUSAN STEPHENS

MILLS & BOON®

First published in Great Britain 2007
Harlequin Mills & Boon Limited,
Eton House, 18-24 Paradise Road, Richmond, Surrey TW9 1SR

© Susan Stephens 2007

ISBN-13: 978 0 263 85388 9

Set in Times Roman 10½ on 12¼ pt
171-0507-47863

Printed and bound in Spain
by Litografia Rosés, S.A., Barcelona

DIRTY WEEKEND

For all the fabulous characters I've met and have yet to meet in the countryside around 'Hawkshead', from a very grateful if mud-splattered townie!

Hugs and happy reading, everyone!

Susan

CHAPTER ONE

As MUD landed on her windscreen the steering wheel jerked out of her hands and Caz Ryan slammed on the brakes. The new silver Mini lurched and slid sideways into a ditch. Everything went black and there was just sound, bad sound, brambles and stone sloughing off showroom-pristine paint and the catastrophic wrenching sound of metal giving way. The car was dead. And now everything had gone eerily quiet.

Careful not to move, Caz conducted a full physical inventory. Everything seemed to be present and correct: no broken bones, no blood dripping on the carpet, she was intact, and, apart from being wedged between her seat and the door with her overnight bag seemingly welded to her head, she was fine. It was a miracle, no thanks to the Neanderthal driving that mud-slinging tractor.

Where was he, by the way? By craning her neck she had a great view of a muddy bank and a road that

belonged under her wheels, not over her head. Her
own fault. She should have stayed in London where
men knew to get out of her way.

In London things were different. She wasn't Caz
Ryan, currently shivering so hard her teeth were
threatening to chip, but Cassandra Bailey Brown, the
über-confident alter ego Caz had created in order to
get ahead.

Finding the name had been easy. Cassandra
because her mother had had a romantic streak—
at least, she had before dumping Caz in a
children's home prior to running away to 'find
herself'. Bailey Brown came out of the phone
book. There were only two listed, which confirmed the surname's exclusivity and made it the
perfect choice.

The reason for the change of name? After leaving
school she hadn't been able to get a job. Her accent
had been a give-away; likewise her manner. She had
known she had to do something and inspiration had
come from the television—newscasters with their
approved English pronunciation were the perfect
people to copy. She had watched, learned and
listened until she'd felt ready to re-launch herself as
Cassandra. The tactic had worked. Doors that had
slammed in Caz Ryan's face were held open by
doormen for Cassandra Bailey Brown.

But Cassandra couldn't help her now. Wriggling
furiously, Caz tried to achieve a better position, but
only succeeded in proving that, whereas Cassandra

walked tall in the city, she couldn't see over the hedge in the country.

However, this was no time for humour. She was shaking so hard she couldn't concentrate. The shock was getting through to her and with it the fact that she was trapped in a car at night and there was no one to help her other than the man she had so rashly overtaken, and who had now disappeared. She couldn't even reach her phone to call for help.

She tried shouting.

The silence was unrelenting and her bravado was being pushed out by fear. Silence in the country was very different from silence in the city; it was all-enveloping, and apart from the wind blowing a horror-movie soundtrack through the trees there was nothing to suggest another human being existed within miles of her.

What if the man drove away? This wasn't London with cars passing every second, this was Hawkshead, last bastion of civilisation before the harsh moorland conditions had deterred even the cavemen.

Caz tensed as a dark shadow loomed over her. 'Don't just stand there! Do something!'

The man didn't move. Maybe he was evaluating the situation, and maybe she was going to pieces. The only certainty was Cassandra's confidence hadn't survived the trip. The man's footsteps crunched away. Brisk and purposeful, they were growing fainter every second. 'Come back here! Don't leave me!'

For a moment she had felt warm beneath his shadow, but now she felt worse than before. She should be appealing to his better nature and not yelling at him. She had caused the accident, after all.

By almost dislocating her neck Caz managed to see out of the car window, but the angle was so acute the most she saw was that the man was some distance away. Although she did notice how tall and lean he was, with powerful shoulders that packed out his rugged jacket. Her body responded with a very different shiver, but had he any intention of helping her?

She had to stay calm. Cassandra never lost control. Cassandra was never lost for direction, let alone in London where everything was so well signed. But here in Hawkshead, miles from her comfort zone, Cassandra was no use at all.

So it was just Caz and the dark and an unknown man. Hugging herself Caz continued to shudder uncontrollably. This was bad news for Cassandra. Cassandra would never shudder. Cassandra was strong. She had recently been appointed a director of Brent Construction in Leeds, one of the top five hundred companies in the country. Cassandra would have to be back all guns blazing in the office on Monday morning when the new chairman was due to take inventory of his board.

Her new boss, Brent junior, had taken a cosy family business and turned it into a world class concern, and rumour said he moved fast to weed out weak links in his chain. Caz accepted business had no heart and didn't expect any favours, but having reached the top of the greasy pole, she had no intention of losing her grip on it.

It was thanks to her alter ego Cassandra that she was here in Hawkshead at all. Cassandra never turned down an opportunity to advance her career, and so Caz had thrown aside the familiar bustle of London for the promise of a better job and a large country house in Yorkshire.

The house in Hawkshead, twenty minutes outside Leeds, was a bonus, a complete surprise, an inheritance from an aunt she'd never met. She'd never been given a thing in her life before, and now a house. Just the thought of it propelled another yell out of her. She couldn't wait to see it; that was why she had come straight from work in Leeds to Hawkshead…

She couldn't hear a thing, other than owls hooting. The feeling of helplessness was new to her, and she hated it, plus she didn't need this aggravation with Monday morning looming large on the horizon.

Twisting her neck again to try and see out of the car, she gasped to see the man was back. He was standing over her holding a giant-sized pair of cutters. For some reason her shivers stopped at the sight of him and a warm throbbing replaced them.

'I've called the emergency services.'

His voice was deep and husky and vibrated

through her. 'Thank you.' Was that her voice shaking?

'And now I'm going to get you out of there…'

She was confident he would, and excitement at the thought flooded through her. She was going to be free. She was going to be freed. *By him.*

As he continued to murmur reassurances there was something in his voice that made her feel younger than Cassandra had felt in a decade.

Caz was only twenty-eight, but she felt eighteen and reckless again, and was glad she'd come straight from the office where Cassandra always dressed to kill. She was still wearing her ridiculously high heels and a too-tight short skirt. Sadly her make-up had endured a long working day followed by a car ride, but she was tearful and vulnerable and ready to be rescued.

She listened intently as he told her how brave she was. She was anything but. She'd spent her whole working life in Human Resources soothing others, bolstering them up, persuading them to take the next step on the ladder, but quite suddenly the tables were turned, and it was she who was floundering. Thanks to her driving the man had assumed she was generally incompetent and was explaining everything he was doing in that low, sexy drawl as if he knew she was on the brink…

Not that she minded listening to him. No…that was like a vocal caress touching every part of her. She was so at ease he made her start when he moved to adjust his position. There was something elemental about him…something he threw off in warm, musky waves. She couldn't even see him properly, but whatever special powers he had, they were curling round her like a seductive cloak.

After a while she relaxed again; the tone of his voice helped. It made him sound like a hero in a film and what was wrong with being the grateful heroine for once, rather than the hard-nosed businesswoman with an attitude towards men?

It took Cassandra to remind Caz that she hadn't battered her way through the glass ceiling to go soft now.

'We're nearly there…'

Caz refocused fast, and as the man dipped his head to speak her body quivered. Her cheeks were tingling too, and she was sure she could feel his warmth brush her face. Every part of her was on full alert, trying to pick up anything she could about him—his accent, his tone, his intentions towards her…

'Are you all right? Not lost your voice, have you?'

There was something warm and humorous in his tone. Caz made a sound to signal her acknowledgement that the man had spoken, but she was soon soothed into silence again by the easy rhythm of his movement. There was an air of purpose and confidence about him, which reassured her. He was probably a builder or a farmer, she guessed. A man used to working with his hands…a man who knew what to do with his hands…a man who would be good with his hands…

She gulped her guilty thoughts back as moonlight streamed in. He had peeled back the roof of the Mini like the lid off a tin of sardines.

'Did you have to do that?' She exploded without thinking. Money was tight, what with the move to Leeds and now her inheritance to lavish luxuries on. She thought back frantically, trying to remember the level of insurance she had taken out on the car.

'Have you got any better suggestions for getting you out?'

The man's tone put her back up. 'You don't know it's safe to move me.'

'You sound well enough to me.'

That sexy drawl could turn hard in a moment, which was quite a turn-on but was he mocking her?

She had to remind herself that up here on the moors the man would come from a traditional community where women knew their place. And that was almost certainly in the kitchen, or his bed… She needed a big gulp of air to consider this.

'There's petrol leaking from your car. I can get you out, or I can leave you here to fry. Your choice—'

What? 'Get me out!' She could smell the petrol now. 'Please!'

'Can you reach your seat belt?'

Before she had chance to reply he had sliced it through with the cutters. His hand brushed hers, an incendiary device carrying with it a thousand messages…strong, warm, dry, smooth, capable being just a few of them.

Her heart was behaving oddly, the rest of her too. She wasn't used to raw masculinity, that had to be it. She was accustomed to boardroom pallor and sandwich bellies. This man's mid-section would be hard and tanned, and banded with muscle…

Caz flinched as a powerful leg clad in well-worn denim brushed her face. He was planting his feet, she realised, straddling the bank above the car, readying himself to lift her out. He manoeuvred with care for such a big man. She caught a glimpse of boots, scuffed and workmanlike, as he lifted her out. And now her face was millimetres from the mud. She recoiled, desperate not to land in it. But then a hand reached around her waist, and she was safe.

'Don't be frightened…'

She was too grateful to be frightened, but her heart was thundering a tattoo. 'Thank you.' He had taken an incredible risk.

'Save it,' he said brusquely, tightening his grip on her.

She could have been cosy in his arms without the tension, but she could feel the sense of danger in him, feel his awareness of it. The car might explode if there was petrol leaking and his desire to put distance between them meant he had no time to waste on superficial courtesies.

She liked that. She liked him. It was an instinctive reaction. She liked being weightless in his arms, and letting him take control. But this feeling of release, of letting go, of allowing someone else to take control, was very new to her. Her job demanded that she was the one who took charge, and as for her life, well, that was the most tightly controlled of all.

Maybe that controlling part of her had got a little out of hand recently, but it stood no chance with this man. She'd never felt like this before, never felt the need to writhe and tangle in a man's arms.

She was allowing her imagination to run away with her, Caz realised and to counteract temptation she immediately went as stiff as a board, which the man answered with some disturbingly intimate pressure in her belly.

'I can't carry you if you're going to turn into a plank of wood.'

Such charm! Such grace! She was right about him being a Neanderthal. But lying in his arms wasn't all bad. She could feel the power in each purposeful stride he took, and, gazing back, she could see the lethal spikes of metal through which he'd threaded her.

They reached a clearing where the moonlight was a little brighter and she could make out the shape of his jaw now. It was strong, firm and black with stubble, which insanely made her long to rub her face against it.

Shock, Caz reasoned, relaxing again. But her gaze crept upwards to study surprisingly sensual lips, set, however, in a grim line that didn't invite fantasy. He was an iron man, she concluded, too primitive for steel, but he was clean. Fresh from the shower, she guessed, he smelled warm and spicy like a hot cinnamon muffin, which reminded her how hungry she was. It was a long time since she had last eaten.

He set off again, carrying her, walking with the poise and natural grace of a man who worked close to the land. She was an expert in people, so she knew. Her new Human Resource director's position meant it was her job to sort out the wheat from the chaff. Cassandra Bailey Brown had made her name sniffing out a candidate's career path before their CV had even landed on her desk. Well, she'd struck lucky this time, Caz thought, because in Cassandra's world it was unusual to find a man who could lift anything heavier than a ring binder, and then only when it was empty.

She was just drifting off into shock-induced torpor again when he suddenly changed his grip.

'Did I hurt you?' he demanded as she exclaimed.

No, but his hand had just connected with her naked butt. Commando was the only option in this skin-tight designer suit. She managed to dredge up enough of Cassandra's *sang-froid* to assure him coolly that she was fine as he set her down.

'Hardly dressed for the country though, are you?' he observed disapprovingly.

Was there a prescribed outfit for landing in a ditch?

With difficulty she held back on the invective that sprang to her lips, making allowances because he had saved her. And she was prepared to admit on this occasion that he was right. Her suit was out of place. But to a workaholic a weekend away meant staying at her desk till the last flicker on her screen. Nevertheless, knickers would have been an advantage tonight. She could still feel his touch branded on her bottom like a quality control stamp.

Caz's heart juddered, and then began to race, as a shaft of moonlight hit her rescuer full in the face. The fading light had robbed the scene of colour, but his eyes seemed to possess a generator all their own. Ocean-green, they were extraordinary against his tan, and his stare was wolf-keen as it rested on her face.

When she stopped quivering enough to think she had to admit that his tan threw her for a moment. Perhaps she'd made a mistake about his profession? No, she thought, reconciling it instead with his outdoor life. She had to have some confidence in her abilities—they had landed her a six-figure salary with the fastest-growing building company on the planet. Trouble was, she'd never met a man like this before. She would have to open a new file at the office marked Miscellaneous Man Hunks.

Caz continued her investigations down long, lean legs and then up again to the somewhat enormous bulge in his jeans.

'Feeling better now?' he said, distracting her.

She quickly refocused, trying to appear calm

when everything inside her was gasping for air. A new kind of shock was setting in, she realised.

The man frowned as he looked at her intently. 'I don't think you're fully recovered yet…'

As he made to pick her up again she backed away. 'No,' she agreed readily, 'I don't think I am, but perhaps if I stand here for a moment…' She fanned herself vigorously to excuse her red cheeks. Her pulse had gone crazy and she had to force her chin to tip to its customary confident angle as he stared at her. Her limbs were trembling beneath his gaze, which was an absolute first for her where men were concerned.

'Don't worry, you'll soon get over it,' he assured her.

She sincerely hoped so.

His long, piercing look was cut short by a call to his mobile. The emergency services, Caz guessed, picking up the command in his tone, which gave her confidence.

'Will they recover the car?'

'I'll keep you updated, don't worry.'

She wasn't sure whether to worry or not at the thought that he intended to keep in touch. Perhaps it would help if he'd just look away while he spoke on the phone, which would give her the chance to reorder her thoughts and reconnect brain synapses that were drifting aimlessly.

Why couldn't she summon up Cassandra when she needed her? This man could be useful, and

Cassandra could spot a promising employee at fifty paces. A competent handyman would be a welcome addition to her staff at Stone Break House, the country seat Caz had inherited. According to her aunt's solicitor it must be somewhere close by, and if this man was local he could show her the way.

She looked at him hopefully as he snapped his phone shut. She felt better just knowing she had the makings of a plan. This might work out for the best, after all. And if it did she would forgive Hawkshead anything…almost anything, Caz amended, cursing fiercely as the heel broke off her shoe.

'Why don't you snap them both off?'

She stared at the man incredulously.

'You'd find it much easier to walk.'

Did he have any idea what these shoes had cost? And if that was humour in his eyes… Caz forced herself to take a few deep breaths. She had to remember what the man had done for her, and what he might still do for her. She couldn't expect him to know the value of luxury products stuck out here in the sticks.

As he held her gaze with a suggestion of amusement in his Cassandra was forced to take a back seat, leaving Caz Ryan to squirm alone. And the squirm started in a place that was normally closed for business as far as men were concerned.

She wasn't used to such directness, Caz reasoned. She wasn't used to men answering her imperative stare with a lazy smile. She wasn't used to lazy smiles setting off quivers down her spine that put some extraordinary thoughts in her head: Lady Chatterley and the gardener; Cassandra and the handyman… Why not? It had a certain ring to it. No one knew her here in Hawkshead; she could do what she liked. But then Cassandra reminded her that there was no time, no place in her life for men.

Which was a shame, Caz thought wickedly, but there was nothing wrong with allowing her fantasies to run free on a country lane. A country lane? In the dark? With a man she didn't know? Nothing wrong? Was she going mad? She would never dream of doing something like this in London or in her new home town of Leeds. So what was different about Hawkshead? What was different about this man?

Drawing herself up to what with her heels should have been an imposing five feet eight, but without them had shrunk to a lopsided five feet three, Caz found herself staring at the third button down on a chequered shirt that was stretched tight over chiselled abs seemingly made out of rock. Maybe if she added some formality to the mix her heart would stop pounding. 'Thank you for your assistance, Mr…?'

'Galem,' he said.

A touch ungraciously, she thought. So was Galem his first name, or his last?

She didn't need to get to know him, Caz reminded herself. Galem was just fine. 'Thank you, Galem. Now, you don't happen to know the number of a local taxi firm, do you?'

He didn't answer her right away, so she took the hint and started digging inside the ridiculously impractical pocket in her jacket where she kept her small change. She breathed a sigh of relief, having found a few coins and a screwed up five pound note. 'Please take this for your trouble,' she said in Cassandra's best ruling class tones.

He ignored her outstretched hand and asked her a question instead. 'And what do they call you in the big city?'

The drawl caught her somewhere between the shoulder blades and then travelled the length of her spine at least twice. 'My name is Cassandra Bailey Brown.' She said this in her best self-tutored voice, and just hearing Cassandra's familiar tones ring out made her feel more confident.

The man looked at her as if she were a species from another planet, then something else crept into his gaze. Was it a spark of recognition? That had to be impossible. Where would their paths ever cross? Cassandra's life was sophisticated, high-tone and fast-paced. This man couldn't even begin to imagine. And now she'd shown her gratitude and her patience was exhausted. For one thing she didn't like being stared at in that faintly mocking way. Wasn't money supposed to be a universal language?

Not here in the country, apparently.

She tried one last time. 'Go on, take it…'

'What for?' he said, frowning.

With a sound loaded with impatience and frustration, she stuffed the money back into her pocket, breaking the last of her acrylic nails as she did so. *Ching!* Her internal till rang again; another fifty pounds down the drain.

'Cassandra Bailey Brown... That's quite a mouthful,' he observed.

As Galem repeated her name Caz noticed how easily a curve of humour found its way to his mouth. He was mocking her again. Cassandra's confident smile evaporated. And why did the name she had chosen for the workplace sound so ridiculous, suddenly?

Maybe because she was plain Caz Ryan?

She couldn't allow him to rattle her. The best employer/employee relationships were based on mutual respect, and first impressions were crucial. 'You haven't told me your second name yet,' she reminded him.

'That's right,' he said unhelpfully. 'My name is Galem. That's all you need to know. And you'll get no taxi here, Cassandra, so what are you going to do?'

Charming! Plus he'd drawn her name out so that Cassandra sounded like some trollop in a porn film. 'Where can I get a taxi then?' she pressed, refusing to be flummoxed.

'Not here...' Slouching on one hip, he looked unhelpful.

'Well, I'll just have to take my chances, and go back to the car. Maybe I'll sleep there,' she said stubbornly, lifting her chin defiantly.

'No, you won't.'

He stepped in front of her. His lazy movements had deceived her. He could move like lightning when he wanted to. 'Are you going to use brute force to stop me?' Even as she suggested it she felt excited.

'If you're daft enough…' He stepped aside.

But as she went to move past him, he nimbly stepped in front of her again. 'I can't let you do that, Cassandra,' he said with the same mocking emphasis on her name. 'In fact, I won't let you do it until the fire service tell *me* the car's safe.' Folding his arms across his chest, he looked down at her, waiting.

'And what am I supposed to do in the meantime?'

'Take a lift with me,' he suggested, easing his massive shoulders in a shrug.

She was certain his dark gaze was mocking her and was equally certain her insides were dancing a tango. She wasn't going anywhere in a car with him; she hadn't lost her marbles altogether.

'Don't worry,' he said with a betraying curve of his lips. 'I'll willingly give you a hand up…'

I bet you would. Her eyes narrowed as she stared back at him, but in truth her options were shrinking.

'Ready?' he said. As he glanced at the tractor and she let out a breath as if she'd been hit in the stomach.

'A lift on your tractor?' she said incredulously.

'Well, I didn't mean on my back.'

The thought of clambering up him without knickers on had to be blanked immediately.

'Are you coming, or not? I promise not to look,' he added dryly.

It was that, or start walking, she realised.

'By the way, you do know this road is a dead end?' he said as she bent down to take off her ruined shoes. 'Where were you going?'

'Of course I know about the road.' She wasn't even sure which road she was on.

'There's only one house down here…'

Her heart leapt. Could this be the right road? Her late aunt's solicitor had told her that Stone Break House was the most substantial house in the village of Hawkshead, and that it stood in solitary splendour at the end of its own road. Solitary splendour, apart from a couple of uninhabited ruins, that was, which she took to mean ruins along the lines of Bolton Abbey, or Fountains Abbey, perhaps with a river running nearby.

Stone Break House represented the pinnacle of Cassandra's aspirations. As far as Cassandra was concerned it said she had arrived. A country seat was what she had been working so hard for ever since Caz had created her. Now Cassandra could keep up, not just with the Joneses, but with the double-barrelled Joneses. The fact that Galem had heard of the house puffed her up even more. Stone Break House…the name alone was enough to thrill her; it had such a ring to it. Caz made a slight, if significant pause before telling him, 'I know it's the only house on the road, because Stone Break House belongs to me now.'

'It does, does it?' He couldn't have sounded more unimpressed.

A tense silence followed.

'Well, come on, then,' Galem said at last in a voice that had lost its charm.

What business was it of his, anyway? Caz thought, wrinkling her brow. Why should he care if she owned the house or not. She shouldn't have told him.

'Shall I leave you here?' he said impatiently.

There were no streetlights in the country, and night had fallen like a smothering black web. The lane was lined with creaking trees and, though she wasn't nervous at night in a brightly lit city, night time in Hawkshead was a very different matter. Stone Break House was sure to be located down some long, impressive drive, and if she missed the gates in the dark and kept on walking into the hills… People had been known to get lost, or eaten by spectral cats, according to some of the magazines she'd read, but, anyway, they definitely disappeared without trace.

'That's it,' Galem said. 'If you can't make your mind up, I'm going.'

'No, wait.' Caz used Cassandra's imperious tones. It was time to re-establish her authority, and Cassandra Bailey Brown had a way with men. In fact one hundred and fifty of them had worked under her in London, something that gave endless amusement to her friends. As they never tired of pointing out, she had one hundred and fifty men working under her, and not one of them had made it on top yet.

'Where men are concerned, you, Cassandra Bailey Brown, are a lost cause…'

And Caz Ryan wasn't much better. As she started to run after Galem, Caz realized this was no time for standing on her dignity. In the city Cassandra might have got her through closed doors that would never have opened for the real Caz Ryan, but in Hawkshead Cassandra was no use to her. It was tempting to think that one day she might put her alter ego in the recycle bin for good. Men had never figured in Cassandra's remorseless drive to the top. So what if she didn't have a private life? She had a blue-chip salary, didn't she? This was the way Cassandra thought. So what if her London chums thought her weird because she didn't date? Truth was one disastrous relationship had been enough for her; it had almost taken her eye off the ball and allowed someone else to be promoted over her head. Cassandra had cut it off without a flicker of remorse long before it had reached the bedroom. The end result? Caz was still a virgin.

'Last chance, townie…'

Slouched on one hip and leaning against his beat-up tractor, Galem was staring at her. 'I'm out of here,' he added, emphasising his point by resting one massive boot on the step of his cab.

'No, wait…please.' She added a plaintive note to her voice, swallowing her pride in the interest of her pedicure. Bare feet and country lanes were a recipe for disaster. 'If you could just drop me off at the gates…'

'The gates?'

'To Stone Break House,' she said as if he should know.

Galem's expression was hidden from her as he came round to help her up. It was this unexpected politeness that stalled her brain for a moment. 'Just as far as the gates will be fine,' she told him, suddenly feeling she maybe shouldn't be alone with him.

'Very well, m'lady,' he said in a way that reassured her.

Perhaps there was hope for him yet, Cassandra approved.

CHAPTER TWO

'THAT'S it?' CAZ peered in horror down the narrow strip of land lit by Galem's tractor beam. This had to be the wrong place. 'You've made a mistake,' she said confidently.

'No mistake.'

'But this can't be Stone Break House. It looks more like a quarry.' She swallowed hard, gazing up at ugly scars carved into the hillside. The peeling sign over what remained of the gates suddenly took on new meaning for her. 'Stone Break House,' she muttered under her breath. 'I see…'

'There's been a quarry here since—'

'Spare me the detail. I'm thinking…' How long had Aunt Maud been in the nursing home? It was hard to be sure since she hadn't even known she'd had an Aunt Maud until the solicitor had tracked her down.

'What are you thinking?' Galem prompted.

'I'm trying to evaluate the potential of my inheritance, actually.' And that was the least of it!

Instead of sympathy or concern a very attractive crease appeared in the side of Galem's beard-roughened cheek as he stared up at the house and his gaze had a faraway look as if he were already picturing the pitfalls she would face if she were foolish enough to attempt a restoration project.

'Someone had a sense of humour leaving you this,' he said, though his own mouth had set into a grim line as if the humour in the situation had bypassed him.

Caz had to admit that Aunt Maud's intentions were a mystery to her. The solicitor had told her that her late mother hadn't spoken to her aunt for years, to the extent that Maud hadn't even known Caz had grown up in an orphanage. Having managed to track her down, Maud had changed her will accordingly. On hearing the news and with no emotion to cloud the picture Cassandra had immediately pictured herself in gaiters and deerstalker hat entertaining her London friends. But as Caz looked at the house now she just felt sad. She could feel the house pulling her in, as if laughter had rung there at one time, and a family had lived and thrived.

She discounted the feeling. Ghosts calling to her? She was still suffering from shock after the accident. But her feelings towards the house made Caz wonder if Cassandra had drifted further away than she thought. Did the country have this effect on everyone?

Not Galem, she gathered, risking a glance at his

glowering face. She wouldn't share her feelings with him. He would only laugh and tell her she wasn't up to the task.

She thanked him for the lift and mentioned the car again; she didn't want to be trapped here.

'When it's recovered I'll let you know,' he said in that weary way men had when a request was repeated.

Leaning across the cab, he opened the passenger door for her. Automatically she pressed back in the seat. She didn't want to get any closer to him than she had to, and she certainly didn't want to become an object of fascination to those piercing sea-green eyes. Galem saw far too much as it was.

He was having a very strange effect on her. Caz could only describe it as the 'bird in her chest' syndrome, and it was growing worse by the minute, and as if that weren't bad enough she couldn't get the bulge in his jeans out of her mind. How did women go on with a thing like that? Surely you'd have to lead up to it? Would she need to be prepared? She had no idea.

It hardly mattered as she wouldn't be finding out, Caz told herself sensibly.

'I guess seeing this must have put you off for life…'

As Galem shouldered the driver's door open Caz almost tumbled out of the cab in her hurry to get away from him. Only when he jumped down after her did she rationalise her thoughts and realise that he had been staring out at Stone Break House when he'd made the comment.

'Not at all,' she shouted back at him, staggering on the uneven ground.

'Why didn't you wait for me?' he said gruffly, appearing at her side. 'I would have helped you down.'

And have him feel her naked butt again? Caz smiled Cassandra's most insincere smile and said nothing. 'Do you have my bag?' she said, remembering it. It was important to her. It was crammed full with every type of beauty product you could think of, plus a bottle of Krug, which her London friends had kindly had delivered to the Leeds office to celebrate moving into her country home.

'Your bag?'

Galem raked his fingers through his hair as if he was having trouble remembering what he'd done with it, but then he brightened up.

'I threw it in the back with the paving slabs,' he said, his voice laced with amusement.

Caz didn't dare to speak. Her brain formed the words, but there was no possible way she could allow her mouth to speak them, not if she wanted to keep Galem on side.

'For safety,' he explained, plonking it down at her feet like a well-trained gun dog.

She didn't want to risk grinding her porcelain veneers and so she decided to forgive him this once and do a little prying. 'So, you're a paver?'

'Something wrong with that?' His mouth turned grim as he held her stare.

'No, of course not,' she lied hastily.

He was standing very close, and it was impossible to miss the fact that his thumbs were lodged in his belt loops pointing the way to his bulging button fly. She quickly looked away, but not before Galem caught her looking. 'I thought you were a farmer,' she said, to excuse her red cheeks.

'Toiling on the land?' he said with irony.

The expression in his eyes shot heat to every part of her. 'That's right.' She formed her lips into a tight line of disapproval. It didn't do to get too familiar. Plus she had a sigh to hold in.

As she refused to meet his gaze she allowed hers to slip, taking in the wide spread of Galem's shoulders and the hint of black chest hair beneath the open buttons on his shirt. The thought of that scratching her—

'Are you all right?'

'Perfectly.'

'You still seem a little shaky to me,' he observed, working his jaw as he thought about it.

'Shaky? Not a bit.' She pulled herself round quickly. 'Thank you once again for tonight…' She turned to go. 'Don't forget to let me know about the car…'

'Nagging woman' appeared in neon lights above his eyes; at the same time he said, 'Sure.'

'Tomorrow?' she said, refusing to be daunted. 'Before lunch.'

'You're not going to be sleeping here tonight.'

His remark sounded dangerously like an order. 'Of course I am.'

Thick black brows drew together over eyes that had suddenly turned a darker shade of green. 'You're kidding me, right?'

'No. I'm perfectly serious.' Swinging her bag onto her shoulder, she reached out to open the gate. 'Thank you again, Galem. See you tomorrow as arranged.' She pushed against it but the gate refused to budge. She kept her cool and tried again, throwing her weight against it this time.

'Too proud to ask for help, Cassandra?'

Caz's jaw set. She tried again. And again. Until Galem took matters into his own hands and leaned across to open it for her. He smelled so good—good enough to eat.

Douse that thought, Caz told herself firmly, flashing him a grateful glance. Galem was a working man, and one who could prove useful if she played her cards right.

Caz walked through the gates towards what she could now see was around six thousand square feet of crumbling ruin. No way was she turning back, but there was no getting away from the fact that Stone Break House was definitely not the manor to which Cassandra had hoped to become accustomed.

'If you intend camping out here I think you'd better take my number,' Galem said.

He was standing somewhere behind her. She

guessed by the gate. She was at the foot of the steps now and had no intention of turning round to see his smug expression.

'I can take you back to the village, if you like?'

He sounded hopeful. Too hopeful. 'I don't like. I'll be fine.'

'This is enough to put anyone off...'

But not me, Caz thought stubbornly. Galem was blatantly trying to persuade her to turn tail and run. Why? 'I'm not put off,' she said, turning to show him her determined face. 'And I'm not hesitating either, I'm simply evaluating the situation.'

'Well, don't take too long about it,' Galem advised with a distinct smile in his voice.

The more certain he sounded that she would take fright, the more Caz became convinced that this was where she belonged, and that Stone Break House needed her. 'There's really no need for you to stay,' she said pointedly.

'Okay,' Galem agreed. 'But before I go I'd better give you my number—'

'Why?' So he could rescue the little woman, no doubt. And if he was local she didn't need his number, she could find it in the phone book. 'If you give me your name I can look you up if I need you.' If there was a patronising note in her voice he deserved it.

He gave it to her anyway, writing it on a scrap of paper with a pen he extracted from his pocket. He came right up to the door and then leaned against the wall to write, giving her ample opportunity to admire his tight buttocks clad in work-distressed jeans.

'Enjoy,' he said, with a last glance at the house before pressing the paper into her hand

'Don't worry, I will,' she assured him. Swinging her bag off the ground, she attempted to appear nonchalant as she secured the strap on her shoulder and her knees threatened to buckle beneath the weight.

'Are you sure I can't help you with that before I go?'

He was still draped casually against the wall. She wished he would go so that she didn't have to do any of this in front of him. 'No, thank you, I can manage.'

He was in two minds, but in the end he let her struggle. If she wanted to wave the feminist banner in his face, so be it. He'd allow her a honeymoon period; he could afford to. What did he have to lose?

Easing away from the damp stone, Galem added, pointing to his list of things to do. He turned to stare back at the house as he walked down the path and tried to feel nothing. He couldn't. How could he when the new owner was just about to step inside? He looked at her. Up. Down. And back again to the determined chin and the firm lips. She would be a hard nut to crack. He looked forward to it.

He was swamped with feelings, some of which he wasn't proud of. Trouble was, the old place meant more to him than bricks and mortar. It was a symbol of his father's struggle. Stone Break House encapsulated something his father had said to him when he'd been starting out. If you didn't care you didn't win. It was a simple philosophy he had taken to the nth degree. It had always served him well, though, perversely, caring as he did had given him the reputation of being hard. And maybe that was true. He didn't want people who didn't care around him.

It was the same with Stone Break House. He cared, and he knew for certain that the new owner couldn't care half as much. He'd planned his tactics well before tonight. His strategy was simple. He would humour the new owner, and then buy her off. But then Cassandra Bailey Brown had landed in a ditch in her silly little suit and high-heeled shoes, and everything had changed when he'd yanked her from the car.

How long would she last? He glanced at her again. He knew what was waiting for her in the house; he'd had a preview. Knowing that meant he couldn't just leave her; he had to be sure she was safe.

He reached the shadows of the outbuildings and chose a spot where he could see everything that was happening at the front door. She was battling with the padlocks. It hurt him to see the place chained. The solicitor had insisted the place was locked up tight, but that hadn't stopped him climbing in through a window. Brushing a hand across his eyes,

Galem grimaced. Feelings as strong as these were inconvenient—they clouded the brain.

The chains fell to the ground. She pushed them to one side and opened the door. The house had fallen so quickly into disrepair he could hardly believe it, and it carved a wedge out of his heart just to see it neglected like this. He was impatient to get started, to buy it from her and restore it. He wouldn't rest until it burst with life again.

She turned around before stepping inside, almost as if she sensed his presence. Or maybe she was having second thoughts. He might have brightened if he hadn't been so concerned. He didn't want her to hurt herself. He should go to her, go round with her and help her, but that would make it too easy for her, and she might decide to keep the house. He couldn't risk it. He just had to stand here and wait for her to break. Wait for the scream…

'Double two, nine five seven triple zero…' Every part of her was tense, but at least she hadn't resorted to a wussy scream. Yet.

Caz listened, and then groaned when she heard the familiar voice of the local butcher. She'd already got him to the phone once already. She made her apologies and tried again. 'Double nine two five seven triple zero…' No, that was someone else's fax machine…

Galem, Galem, Galem. Cursing softly, Caz redialled. She resented Galem climbing inside her head, but he was the only person she knew to call. And she couldn't find the scrap of paper he'd given her. She'd glanced at it, and then stuffed it in her pocket, but now she couldn't find it. Still, her brain should work, shouldn't it?

Dithering about wasn't like her and neither was forgetfulness, or spiders the size of dinner plates and nests of mice in the bath. 'Bath!' Caz exclaimed to the empty room, running a distracted hand through her designer do.

Pacing the floor, she glared at the phone in her hand. If there'd been any hot water at Stone Break House, any water at all, or even one room with a door or ceiling intact… The list of disasters went on and on. She guessed tiles must have come off the roof and the rain had got in, and after that it was a short journey to disaster—rafters collapsing, systems failing. And now it was pitch black outside and she had no light other than the screen on her phone, and that would soon run out of battery. Added to which, she had no heat, no food, no sanitation, and nowhere to sleep—short of curling up in the bath with the mice, of course.

But she did have that fortune of beauty preparations, which she had brought with her in anticipation of some serious self-indulgence, Caz remembered, taking a well-aimed kick at her designer bag.

Brushing up against the suspiciously furry walls, she shuddered. Stone Break House stank of damp and decay. It was a prize-one example of a dump, and she knew a lot about dumps. But even the children's home had been a palace in comparison to this. So why did she feel so determined to restore the place? How was it she could picture Stone Break House becoming a place where people would feel warm and welcome?

She laughed into the silence. Impossible tasks were her speciality, weren't they? Or, at least, they were Cassandra's. There wasn't a problem at work Cassandra couldn't get around. But this… Caz shuddered and tried to feel brave.

Double two five nine seven triple zero… 'Yes!' It was ringing, but, so far, no reply. How many more chances would she have before her battery went flat and she was alone in the dark? If only she could remember Galem's number. She started chomping on what was left of her nails. Cassandra wouldn't have lost the number. Caz Ryan, however, had been too busy drooling over the gorgeous man as her body had prepared for some high octane fantasy adventures.

CHAPTER THREE

SHIFTING the phone to her other shoulder, Caz occasionally shuddered as she brushed imaginary spiders off her jacket. The trouble was, even if she got through to him she just had to hope Galem knew the number of a local guest house...

'Galem?' She brightened, hearing his voice. 'Galem, is that you? Galem!' Caz shrieked, clutching her chest. Galem was standing right behind her! 'How did you get in?' she shouted, angry that he'd surprised her.

'The door was open...' He flashed a torch in her face.

'Turn that off. All right, turn it on again.' Better to be blinded than blind-sided; she wanted to keep track of him. She was in the middle of nowhere at night in a ruined house with no means of summoning help if things turned awkward with a man she didn't know.

She refused to listen to the inner voice assuring

her that Galem wasn't the pouncing type. She had been dragged up in the school of hard knocks and knew you could never take anything for granted. 'How did you know I would need you?' she said suspiciously.

'Now let me see,' he said dryly, looking around.

She had inadvertently massaged his male ego. Big mistake. 'There's nothing here I can't handle— Okay,' she admitted when his lips tugged up with amusement, 'I'm glad you're here.'

His gaze moved to her mouth and settled there.

'Yes, I'm glad to see you,' she said, pressing her lips together to hide how plump they felt, 'because things aren't quite as I expected them.' The truth was she had never needed Galem's solid presence more. He was a dragon slayer—a mouse would be nothing to him. The temptation to throw herself into his arms and seek shelter from all the as-yet-unidentified monsters in the house was overwhelming, but fortunately with the effect he was having on her she had more sense.

'Does the house scare you?'

He wanted her to be scared. He wanted her to admit she was wrong and ask him to take her to the nearest station.

She wanted to be brave, more than anything she wanted to prove her courage, but here amongst the creatures who had taken up residence in her house she was an unrepentant coward. 'I'm not scared,' she said, pulling a face. 'What on earth made you think that?'

'Let's call it intuition, shall we?' he drawled in a way that made her shiver.

Let's not! She didn't want him reading her mind. 'You haven't told me yet why you came back.'

'I thought I'd better check up on you.' His brow wrinkled as he stared up at her through a dark fringe of lashes. 'You sounded pretty strung out when I walked in. What's up?'

What's up? Couldn't he see? 'Could you lower that torch, please?'

As he did so he then tapped it against his thigh, drawing her gaze to the very place she knew she mustn't look. She dragged her gaze away, relieved when Galem straightened up and walked away a few paces to lean his weight against a supporting beam.

'I've always loved ancient structures,' he murmured, caressing it.

As she heard her ragged sigh creep out Caz had to wonder if she was jealous of a beam now. She had to tell him the truth. The longer she waited to do so, the harder it would get. 'Galem, I'm going to need your help.' Was that a little smile of satisfaction? Caz wondered. If it was it couldn't be helped. She did need him. There was no point in allowing her pride to stand in the way of a sensible decision.

'I can see that,' he said with an annoying degree of assurance.

Humility clearly wasn't his style, Caz conjectured. She pressed on. 'We can both see the house is a wreck, and I need to see a way forward—'

'Why? Why don't you just sell it—let someone else do the worrying?'

Because she wanted to. And why was he so quick off the mark with that suggestion? Did Galem want the house for himself? She pushed that thought away; it was too ridiculous. What would he do with a house of this size?

'I'd just sell it, if I were you.'

Oh, would you? she thought grimly. But then she welled with emotion, which she hadn't expected. The house touched something deep inside her. She couldn't even fully explain why to herself, so the chances of explaining why to Galem were nil.

He touched her arm lightly as if he sensed the way she felt, but she knew he didn't want her here. She could feel it. She could also feel her heart turning somersaults just because he'd touched her, which was very inconvenient.

What he couldn't know was that that consoling pat was one of the most intimate touches she had ever received. That was the trouble with emotional starvation—you never knew where boundaries lay. Sometimes as a child she used to think she would even exchange the rag doll she'd made in sewing class for a hug.

And there was something about Galem's touch, even that impersonal touch. His fingers had slid down her arm from shoulder to elbow so lightly she'd barely felt them, but it was something to put in her emotional bank and draw on when she needed. Of course Cassandra had shown her lots of ways to feel good about herself, but you couldn't cuddle up to money on a cold night.

'Not so good—'

She jerked to full attention as Galem spoke. He was swinging the torch as he examined the crumbling ceiling, some of which was open to the rafters, she noticed now. 'But all repairable,' she insisted doggedly. If this old house was what it took to make her feel she had a home, she would do anything to restore it. This wasn't a project for her any longer, this was a mission.

To her surprise Galem agreed with her, saying that everything in the house could be made right at a price. That was good news and bad news; she didn't have a bottomless pot of money. 'It's a pity the solicitor didn't warn me so I could have organised a proper loan with the bank.'

'They probably didn't want to frighten you off with a long list of "things to do".'

It was the most reasonable thing he'd said to her—factual and without edge. It made her wish for ridiculous things, like that they could be friends, maybe.

They were standing on opposite sides of a huge divide. She wanted the house as much as he did. There was no resolution to that problem. What he should do was walk away. But he didn't want to.

Instead he wanted something he couldn't have—the house and her. She was feisty and determined, and she touched something inside him.

'You were right, it is a dump,' she said, forcing him to refocus. 'And as for basic amenities?' She was smiling. 'Let's not even go there.'

He laughed. 'Not to mention the décor—'

When Galem laughed it was a rich, warm, engaging sound.

'The Barney Rubble School of interior design,' she suggested.

'You could be right.' He trailed the beam of the torch across the ceiling.

'I've noticed Barney Rubble lives next door,' she said.

'You have?'

As Galem rasped a firm thumb pad across his stubble she was fascinated.

'The cartoon character Barney Rubble,' he prompted.

Humour was tugging at his lips, and a lock of his inky black hair had caught on his lashes. Imagining him stretched out on a sofa watching cartoons made her smile broaden.

Get a hold of yourself, Caz Ryan! Cassandra warned.

'I was given to understand no one else lived on this road,' Caz said on a serious note. 'But there's definitely an old man living in the shack next door.'

'You mean old Thomas?' Resting his weight on

one hip, Galem held her gaze in a way that made her heart pump faster.

'Yes…' Clearing her throat, Caz tried to order her thoughts. 'That must be him.'

From the tone of Galem's voice she gathered 'Old Thomas' was no threat to her. He was surely less of a threat to her than Galem! 'I don't know his name,' she admitted. 'All I know is that I saw an elderly man chasing chickens by torchlight next door…'

'Keeping them at home can't be healthy, can it?'

'Maybe they keep him warm at night…'

The way Galem was looking at her made it impossible not to think what it would be like cuddled up with him in a big, cosy bed. He had a way of staring into her eyes as if he could see everything she was thinking. She quickly looked away again.

'This house is a listed building,' he said, easing the tension by walking away.

'Really?' She was relieved just to breathe again.

'It's going to take a special type of dedication to bring it back to life.'

That sounded very much like a challenge. 'I've got all the dedication it takes.'

Galem's jaw firmed, but he didn't rise to the bait, he just kept on with the *son et lumière* effect he was creating on the ceiling. 'This central area dates back to the sixteenth century…'

'And most of the original dust is still intact,' Caz felt driven to observe. This idea of his that she was incapable of handling the project was getting under her skin.

'Someone loved it once,' Galem murmured.

'And someone will again.'

He turned to stare at her. For a moment she thought he believed her, but then his expression changed.

'I recommend you hoover the walls,' he said, running the flat of one hand across them.

She'd had enough. 'Are you determined to put me off?'

'Not at all…'

But a shudder was already speeding down her spine. What sort of creatures did he suggest lurked between the stones? Caz wondered, screwing up her eyes to stare more closely at them. Unconsciously she gravitated towards Galem, just in case.

They were standing very close now, and as she looked up he looked down. She felt compelled to say something…anything. 'Is the ceiling safe?' How beautiful his mouth looked when he frowned.

'You'll be light enough to walk up there in safety, I expect…'

He expects? What if he proves to be wrong and the floor gives way? Ground floor only, Caz concluded, not that she had the slightest intention of revisiting the upper rooms after her earlier encounter with the mice. With a shrug Galem smiled into her eyes, and she guessed that remark about her weight was probably the closest to a compliment he ever came.

'There'll be woodworm, too, I expect,' he said, shining his torch on the banister leading to the first floor.

'So there's wet rot, dry rot, woodworm, mice and spiders as big as dinner plates—'

'You'd better use earplugs.'

'Earplugs?' Was the house on a flight path? Or in the middle of the army training ground, perhaps?

'To stop anything crawling in while you're asleep…the same with your mouth.'

'And nose?'

'You choose…but I wouldn't recommend both.'

She held her breath as he raised his arm; she was so sure he was going to brush her hair out of her eyes, and her face was already tingling. But then he clutched the back of his neck instead, and looked at the door. She didn't want him to go yet. As if he read her mind he pressed her back against the wall. She was instantly melting, eyes closed, heart—

'Look out!'

Heart stopping! Caz's eyes flashed open at Galem's warning, and then she screamed. Far from being the prelude to a romantic moment pushing her back against the wall had been to move her out of the way of a troupe of marauding mice. She hated mice. They moved even faster than spiders!

Without thinking what she was doing Caz launched herself at Galem. Locking her hands around his neck, she cried into his chest. 'I thought I could handle this…'

Her voice was muffled, which made her seem more vulnerable than ever, and her breath was warm against him. He couldn't remember the last time he'd felt like this—the last time anyone had clung to him like this. 'There's no shame in admitting you were wrong,' he told her.

'I'm not wrong,' she retorted stubbornly. 'I just need time to get used to things here.'

His face was buried in her hair. He inhaled deeply. She smelled so good, like wildflowers in a summer meadow. 'That's quite a colony of mice you've got there.'

'I'll get used to them, too,' she lied, clutching her chest.

'Get real… You can't stay here overnight. I won't let you.'

'You can't stop me—'

He put up his hand before she could get into the feminist issues again. 'I wouldn't stay here. Is that good enough for you? Plus, you've had one bad shock tonight, you don't need more.'

She gazed around and he could tell she was coming round.

'I can look after myself, you know.'

'I never doubted it, but not here, not tonight. While I'm here why not take advantage of me?'

He saw the flicker in her eyes. So, she'd like to. But she was still as wary as a doe that hadn't been covered by a buck. Then he saw the answer to the

problem hovering in a corner. 'Hey, look at this…'
One of the little fellers had got left behind.

'What are you going to do with it?' She clutched
her throat.

Walking across the room, he picked up a spade
that had been discarded on top of an old sack, and
advanced on the mouse.

'Don't kill it! *Don't kill it!*' She ran to him and
clutched his arm. The mouse looked helpless
suddenly, frozen in the beam of his torch. Twitching
up the sack, he tossed it over the mouse and sho-
velled it up. 'I'm not going to kill him, don't worry,
I'll take it outside and dispose of it—'

'Don't leave me! *Don't leave me!*' Panic-stricken,
she hobbled after him.

'Okay,' he said in a soothing tone, 'I'll let you
supervise his release.'

Was he mad? He was mad. Caz was shuddering
so badly she had to do a little dance to get over it.
'Wait!' she commanded as Galem ducked his head
to go through the door.

'What?' He stood frozen, arm outstretched, with the
mouse balanced neatly on the shovel beneath the sack.

She almost cannoned into him and had to take a
moment to restore her equilibrium while Galem
lounged back against the door frame, waiting for her.
Even through the grainy miasma of shock he looked
amazing. He was all shoulders and chest, clad in
something darkly Aran, and down from that, skim-
ming some important bits, were those long, lean,

denim-encased legs, tipped with kick-the-door-down boots.

Caz refused to compute what she'd seen on the skim. Galem had very big feet, she concluded. 'I'm ready to help you with the mouse,' she said, in case he was in doubt at all.

Lowering the spade, Galem rested it gently on the ground. 'Just take the sack away, Caz, and then he'll run…'

Something leapt inside her as he called her Caz. It moved through her body until it grabbed something in her stomach and twisted it.

CHAPTER FOUR

MUSTERING all her courage, Caz approached the sack. Plucking up one edge with her fingertips, she sprang back with a sound of revulsion.

The mouse was surprisingly slow on the uptake and surprisingly tiny. It looked straight at her with its bright beady eyes, and then, once it was satisfied that she had no intention of moving, it stared to the left and then the right as if it had reached some mousely crossing before shooting away.

She stood motionless at Galem's side, feeling they'd done the right thing. 'I need somewhere to stay tonight, don't I?' she said frankly.

'Yes, you do,' he agreed, lips tugging up at one corner in a way that made her heart rate quicken.

She narrowed her eyes just to let him know this wasn't a total climb down. 'I'll be back in the morning, of course.'

'Of course.' Galem's mouth settled in a way that

put a crease in his cheek. 'So what did you have in mind for tonight?'

'Somewhere with a ceiling,' Caz suggested. 'And doors would be a bonus.'

'You don't ask for much.'

'There's more,' she told him promptly. 'I want water. Lots and lots of water. And I mean hot, clean, running water, not a stream or a stagnant puddle—'

'And you expect to find all this in Hawkshead?'

The way he dipped his head to tease her ran heat into parts of her that had remained inactive for years, but he was the best hope she had of finding a warm bed for the night. 'All I want is a respectable guest house with hot and cold running water.'

'I'm afraid there aren't any guest houses in Hawskhead. So what do you plan to do now, Cassandra?'

'No guest houses? You're kidding me?'

'I'm perfectly serious,' Galem assured her.

Where had she landed up—Desolation Alley? Her fantasies were slipping down the drain one by one. The big house, living in the lap of luxury, lady of the manor, all that stuff, everything lay in tatters at her feet. Plus the car was a wreck and she was stuck here for the foreseeable future. Great.

Right on cue Caz's stomach rumbled, reminding her how long it had been since she had last seen a plate of food.

Galem raised a brow. He could afford to. He was

warm, clean and confident, while she was starving, freezing and filthy. How had that happened?

She was the executive here, Caz reminded herself, and Cassandra was always immaculate—if not well fed. Cassandra's calorie-conscious diet could scarcely be called satisfying. The thought of rich northern delicacies cascaded into Caz's mind, egged on by the fact that all she'd eaten that day was one low-fat yoghurt and a handbag-size bottle of water purchased from the petrol station. 'There has to be a pub in the village.' She spoke with determination.

'Not one that you can walk to.'

The way Galem was looking at her suggested he was waiting for her to break down and howl. 'Well, can we drive there?' she persisted.

'Possibly.'

'Possibly? What does that mean?' She frowned at him ferociously, brushing aside all the beauty tips she'd ever read about facial expressions encouraging lines.

'There's a possibility I might drive there,' he elaborated.

Well, don't do me any favours! She didn't like the way Galem's lips were tugging up in a predatory way as if he was enjoying every minute of this. 'Does the pub have rooms?' Right now she would have sold her grandmother—if she'd had one—for a lift to the pub, even in Galem's tractor.

'I suggest we go to my place so you can clean up first.'

His place? Not a chance. Was he mad? He was mad, and she already knew that, or why was he here staking his claim to a house they both knew was a wreck? 'I wouldn't dream of putting you out,' she said, trying to keep the sarcasm from her voice.

'You wouldn't be,' he said matter-of-factly.

She broke eye contact to give herself chance to think. She couldn't risk going to his house. 'I'd rather eat first. I'm starving.'

'Fine. I'll take you for dinner.'

Dinner? Could he afford it? She had given him the once-over before she could stop herself. And he'd seen her. 'Don't worry, I'll go Dutch.'

'It won't break the bank…this once.'

The Cassandra in her reacted positively to the suggestion of dinner. The glossies were full of fabulous restaurants tucked away in unsuspected places. 'Well, if you're sure about this…that's very kind of you.'

'You look like you need something inside you.'

Her heart started pumping like a steam train going downhill. She didn't dare contemplate what he meant.

'I know just the place,' Galem said, leading the way to the door. 'The lightest pastry you'll ever eat,' he said, 'and the gravy…' He smacked his lips, drawing her gaze back to them.

It was hard to concentrate and remember that however fragrant and tasty, fat-filled food did not appear on Cassandra's diet sheet. 'Is it a good restaurant?' Caz asked in the faint hope of a Michelin star to ease her conscience.

'The best,' Galem said with a winning smile.

She couldn't hold back a tiny, contented sigh. The thought of food, warmth and Galem was a hint that things were going to turn out better than she had expected. She had already located the nearest salad bar to her office in Leeds, but quite suddenly the idea of counting calories didn't appeal. Cassandra had grown used to the best things in life, and Galem had declared his intention to introduce her to the best of Hawkshead—what more could she possibly ask of him?

Her suit was ruined, and the mouse incident had persuaded Caz to change into an outfit that didn't leave her legs bare. She didn't have much choice in her bag, as she had packed for Cassandra's antici- pated five-star stay.

Rummaging around she found a cashmere track suit, which the assistant in Harvey Nichols had assured her would be perfect for the country. She could change into it in a small pool of light cast by Galem's torch, which he had kindly balanced on top of a crumbling wall for her before politely turning his back. She didn't want to risk any member of the animal kingdom community running up her legs, and nor did she want to linger a moment longer than she had to at Stone Break House in its present con- dition.

She had no option but to trust Galem, Caz thought as she pulled off her clothes, and she didn't want to let him go, not yet. She wanted him, the house needed him; right now she needed him to show her the ropes in the village. But at the same time she felt naked and vulnerable with so much man standing by. She could hear him breathing in the stillness. She could sense his presence like some mighty power source. Being close to him felt good, especially in the dark in the country, and especially under these circumstances…under any circumstances.

'Are you ready yet?'

Was she ready? Galem's promise of crisp golden pastry and rich, succulent gravy made Caz race into action. Plucking out the first pair of briefs she came to in her ruined designer bag, she wriggled her nakedness into them. They were skimpy see-through red lace. All her underwear reflected a life full of sin and sex. She might be virginal, but that was no excuse for white cotton, and her lingerie was anything but.

'Hurry up!'

She drew in a fast breath as Galem shifted position, but a discreet check proved he hadn't turned around. She hurried to make herself decent, and pulled on the final part of her ensemble, a fabulous two-ply cashmere hoodie.

'Only we don't want to give old Thomas a heart attack, do we?'

She whirled around in time to see 'Old Thomas' raise his bony hand in greeting.

'Not good for his blood pressure…'

'You knew he was there?' She threw a furious stare at Galem.

'You knew he lived next door. It was you who told me about him.'

'There is no next door!'

With a huff of frustration Caz touched a hand to her forehead, trying to block out the reality that had so quickly overtaken her fantasy. 'Okay, there is someone living next door,' she conceded. 'Old Thomas lives next door, and I will remember to be more careful in future…' This was an instruction for herself, and not for Galem.

'I'm hungry, too,' he complained, drawing her attention to his super-flat belly with a pat, 'and if you want to arrive before the food runs out I suggest you get a move on…'

A restaurant where the food ran out? It had to be exclusive. Stuffing the rest of her things in the bag, she hurried down the path after him.

'Are you sure you don't want to go back to my place first?' he said when they reached the gate.

'I'm quite sure.' She was in no hurry to see *his place.* She knew better than to risk her safety with a man she didn't know, and, had she been feeling reckless, a scruffy bachelor pad—there was no ring on his finger, she'd checked—was hardly a draw. Plus, she had a plan. When they arrived at the up-market restaurant she would ask around. Surely someone would know if anyone in the village took in paying guests. She was prepared to pay double whatever anyone asked for the simple luxury of a clean bed and a hot shower.

'The village hall…' It wasn't a question, more a resigned statement of fact.

Michelin star? The Cassandra in her raged inwardly. Are you crazy? Restaurant? Cassandra sneered rather unpleasantly this time. Forget it!

It was hardly the smart wine bar she was used to, Caz had to admit. Plus, from the sound of it there was a well-attended hoe-down underway. Brace yourself, Caz's inner voice under the instruction of Cassandra commanded. She'd just keep thinking about the golden pastry and rich succulent gravy, Caz decided, adopting a brave expression. Or was that one of Galem's tall stories too?

'I take it you like line dancing?' he said, mistaking her smile.

'Line dancing?' Caz's jaw dropped in horror. But then Galem turned his face to the porch light. It was the first time she'd got a proper look at him. She'd been freezing in the brisk north wind moments earlier, but now she was blazing with feelings so intense she would have welcomed a snow shower to cool her down. Galem wasn't just good-looking, he was phenomenally good-looking. He was the rough, tough alpha women obsessed over. And she had sexual needs she had never acknowledged before. Luckily she was standing in the shadows where she could self-combust unseen.

'Line dancing?' Galem prompted, offering her his arm.

It took her brain a moment to click into gear. And then she had to remind herself that Hawskhead was in the countryside where people had different interests from people who lived in the city. They were lucky, Caz told herself sternly, and if she only opened her eyes she might find a world waiting for her in Hawskead. The first of those opportunities was standing right in front of her.

'You can stand outside in the cold,' Galem said, lounging against the door jamb, 'or you can come inside with me.'

Caz didn't need much persuading, and was deeply conscious of the difference in their sizes as Galem nudged the door open with the toe of his boot. When he offered her his arm a second time she took it. They were only role-playing; there was no harm in it. She was safe.

His arm felt warm and strong and she barely reached his shoulder. Through the open door, she could smell the warm gravy and it made her mouth water, though the scent of warm, clean man was just as appetising. Closing her eyes, she inhaled deeply. The better to appreciate it.

'Hot hash?'

Galem was speaking very close to her ear and his warm breath made her neck tingle. 'Can I eat it?'

Opening her eyes wide, she looked up at him. She was flirting with him, Caz realised. And this time Galem didn't take the opportunity to tease her, he just looked straight back into her eyes and held her gaze so she could see his eyes darken. Her heart juddered and missed a beat when his glance moved on to her lips. She hadn't thought him interested, not even remotely. She was melting from the inside out, and heat was coiling round her hips. 'Can I?' she whispered, having forgotten the question.

'If you like,' Galem murmured very close to her lips.

His cheek had creased again. 'It might lead to something more,' he warned.

'Really?'

Her eagerness made him smile. 'Yeh, like a chassé and a lock step shuffle…'

He was talking about dancing. She wasn't sure whether to be disappointed or relieved.

'Well?' he prompted. 'Are we going to stay here on the doorstep all night, or are you going to take a chance in the hall?'

Caz looked past him to where she could see people milling around. Taking her hesitation as assent, Galem held the door open for her. As she walked through it his tanned fist was only just inches from her face. It made her belly hot to think of that strong hand unfurling to trace the lines of her body.

She welcomed the distraction of a packed hall. There was barely room to move, and she was shoved up against Galem, which felt good, excellent to have him at her side like a rock defending her. The dancing had begun and everyone seemed to know the steps. She felt a ripple of alarm. She hoped she wouldn't be put to the test. She was a hopeless dancer. 'When do we eat?'

'You have to dance first.'

'What do you mean?' Caz looked at him in alarm.

'I mean you have to dance first to earn your supper.' He shrugged, apparently unaware of her sudden attack of nerves.

'You can't be serious?'

'Why not?'

'You are.'

'I am.' His lips tugged up, proving yet again how much he enjoyed her discomfort. Well, if he was trying to scare her off he'd failed again.

'It's too late to change your mind now.' His green eyes were dancing with laughter. 'Courage,' he said. 'I'll be with you every step of the way.'

CHAPTER FIVE

THE temperature inside the village hall was approaching tropical, and Caz was in the wrong outfit again. No one else seemed to care that their cheeks were rosy red and heat radiated off the walls—they were all far too busy strutting their stuff. It surprised Caz to see how much trouble people had gone to with their outfits, so many of them were wearing stetsons, cuffs and boots, and when Galem tugged off his Aran sweater she saw he was wearing a dark shirt, which, with his snug-fitting jeans and rugged boots, made him look the part.

'No stetson, sorry,' he said dryly when she looked at him, but from the expression in his eyes Caz deduced Galem didn't have a sorry bone in his body. But at least he fitted in. Fitted in? Galem looked great. He would have fitted in anywhere from Rodeo Drive to the village hall. And when he rolled back the sleeves of his shirt and she saw the size of his arms she nearly fainted.

SUSAN STEPHENS 65

She was still frozen to the spot when he caught hold of her hand and tugged her with him through the crowd. It was then she saw another sight that made her gasp. Resplendent in a yellow jump suit and with his wild grey hair tamed and swept back beneath a Brylcreme sheen, Old Thomas was mounting the steps at the side of the stage with a guitar slung over his shoulder.

Galem was ready to dance from the moment he hit the floor, and had none of her inhibitions. Soon everyone was dancing; except for her. She had spent too long as Cassandra Bailey Brown to let go now. The mould had set around her and she didn't know how to break free. Being jostled, feeling awkward and getting hotter by the minute, Caz was dreading the moment when Galem made her dance. She couldn't dance. She didn't know how. She had never learned. She'd never had the opportunity to learn.

'Come on,' Galem insisted. 'Let's see what you're made of.'

She rose to the challenge, tipping her chin and this time ignoring the helping hand he stretched out. But she was tempted. Holding Galem's hand wasn't something you easily forgot, and the truth was she wanted her hand back in his. His hand had felt warm and sure, and she liked the roughness of it against her soft skin. He was a working man; who wouldn't be turned on by that?

He led her past a raised platform where a team of nubile lovelies clad in little more than white fringed bandages and high-heeled boots were demonstrating the finer points of each dance. They paused as Galem passed by and all of them fluffed a step. He stared back, Caz noticed, openly winking! Brazenly smiling! She stalked ahead. He belonged to her. Or, at least, she was on the point of taking him on as her official handyman and caretaker at Stone Break House. In her mind his services were already booked for the foreseeable future. And when he worked for her she would not permit any distractions. 'When do we eat?' she said, feeling grumpy. 'I've had enough of this—'

'Already?' Galem's lips tugged down in mock concern and there was laughter in his eyes. 'If you've had enough already I'm afraid you won't eat tonight. And I thought you had more guts, Cassandra…' His voice had hardened.

'More than you know.'

'The rules are strict here,' he told her with too much satisfaction. 'They go something like this: no dancing; no eating.'

'Fine.' She glared at him, wondering whose rules he was talking about. 'Let's dance.'

He dragged her close and suddenly her bravado deserted her. The trouble was he felt so good she couldn't think, and when she couldn't think her feet went everywhere. 'I can't do it,' she said impatiently. 'I just can't.'

'Everyone can dance. You just have to let yourself go.'

Could she just *let go?*

'Come on, follow me. I'll help you.'

Galem was still holding onto her, and she was still wanting him to hold onto her—anywhere but on a dance floor.

'I can't—'

'Yes, you can.' And to prove it he held her closer still so she had no option but to move with him.

'No, I can't, and I don't want to.'

'Is that why your foot's tapping in time to the music? I did wonder. Who cares if you make a fool of yourself?'

Caz had rather hoped Galem might.

'Are you afraid to break the mould for one night?'

His question was too close to the truth to answer.

They stood without moving for a moment on the centre of the dance floor. Galem's warmth was flooding through her; she could feel it in every fibre of her being. Could she let go this once? Could she let go enough to dance with Galem? She glanced up, only to see his face crease in the familiar grin again. She looked away quickly, conscious that her face was already burning. Old Thomas was singing his heart out. What was wrong with her? Wasn't Hawkshead supposed to be an escape from Cassandra? Or was she inviting her to take over every part of her life?

'I'm not standing here all night,' Galem said.

'Sorry, I just needed a moment.'

'A moment? You've had half an hour.'

He made her smile. She needed more than a moment to get over the way Galem made her feel.

'You can't resist this music,' he said as the infectious rhythm gathered pace.

'Well, it's hard to ignore it when it's playing at twenty decibels.' The best she could hope for was to jig about in her clumsy way and try not to tread on him. But then reprieve came in the shape of a trolley loaded with plastic cups and orange juice.

'Better grab a drink while we can,' Galem advised. 'Orange squash?'

He had to ask twice because she was looking at his lips…his beautiful, *beautiful* lips. And then she had to do a quick reality check: Cassandra/London wine bar/Chardonnay. Caz Ryan/Hawkshead village hall/orange squash. 'Thank you, I'd like that.'

Lifting a giant-sized jug, Galem poured her a glass. She was so thirsty, and the orange squash was refreshing and delicious. Cramming a handful of the crisps he offered into her mouth, Caz studied the lines of dancers. They were jigging away without partners like cowboys of old who had felt the need to dance, but not with each other.

And in a mirror there was Caz Ryan hovering; no confidence at all. It reminded Caz of her need for Cassandra and of the fact that she had only ever been successful as Cassandra. Caz Ryan never tried new things, because she knew before she did so that she would fail. Caz Ryan didn't expect anything from life, or from anyone, except Cassandra; Cassandra had never let her down.

But Cassandra wouldn't be standing here on the edge of the dance floor in Hawkshead village hall trying to decide whether or not to join the party, Caz reminded herself impatiently. Cassandra had been left outside the door.

'Are you ready to walk the line, Caz?' Galem said, taking the plastic cup from her hand.

Concentrating fiercely, she nodded her head.

To begin with it was a disaster. Each time she thought she knew what she was doing and took a firm step everyone shot off in the opposite direction. Galem had no such difficulty, he had obviously been born to dance. He had a natural rhythm and, far from making a fool of himself, was attracting a lot of attention. An admiring circle had soon formed around him. Caz longed to retreat to the sidelines, but Galem wouldn't let her. Each time she tried to sidle towards the edge of the dance floor he brought her back. She stumbled left and stumbled right, and nearly fell into him at one point. She could run or she could get a grip of this… Tearing off her hoodie she saw Galem watching her out of the corner of her eye. He was waiting to see what she would do. Well, he'd find out. She was going to be the best dancer there if it killed her.

Or not!

Caz jumped a mile as Galem's hand landed on her shoulder.

'What are you doing?' He had to bring his face close to ask the question above the noise and she could see the humour in his eyes.

'I'm dancing.' But what was he doing, was more to the point. His hand was sliding slowly down her arm, drawing her towards him and provoking stampedes of sensation as it went. 'What do you think I'm doing?' she managed faintly. 'You can let me go now…'

'I'm afraid that's not possible.'

'Not possible?' she said, putting up some token resistance. 'Why not?'

'Because this is a couples' dance. Are you normally so confused? I do hope not, Cassandra…'

So did she, Caz thought. She had to relax, and she might as well start now. If she was going to relax anywhere, Hawkshead was the place to do it.

But. Having adjusted his grip, Galem was pressed up hard against her. She could feel every inch of him. She'd never been held like this before by anyone, never been held like this before ever…

'I like it when you look bewildered,' he murmured against her face. 'It's almost as cute as when you dance.'

Cute? No one had ever called her cute before.

'Come with me,' he said.

She hesitated, resisting the tug on her hand. 'Go where?' she said. She had been comfortably nuzzled against his chest and there was nowhere she would rather be…except perhaps alone with him. But then the music changed, spoiling everything. It was too fast, too loud, and the whole place erupted into shouts, stamps and whistles. The one good thing about it was that Galem was forced to sweep her out of the way of the super-efficient chorus line that threatened to mow her down.

'You'll never get the hang of the dancing if you don't pay attention.' He laughed.

At that moment Caz couldn't have cared less about the dancing. She hid her smile. They were almost flirting. She wished she had the nerve to tell him she wanted to get the hang of it. She had never held a man before, and it was something she was keen to investigate further. As he took her hand she went with him willingly, anticipation of what was coming next making her tighten her grip.

But he stopped at the steps where some of the better dancers were performing on a platform. 'Where are you taking me?'

'Up there.'

'Oh, no…'

Galem just grinned, and, putting an arm round her waist, hoisted her up onto the platform.

'I can't do this,' Caz exclaimed when Galem sprang up beside her. 'And you know that.' She turned on her heels, fury propelling her.

He caught hold of her and brought her back. The last thought in his mind was to humiliate her. Maybe it had been in his plans at one time. At first he'd considered all sorts of plans to drive her away. But in the past hour he'd realised how unhappy she was. Beneath her Cassandra Bailey Brown brittle shell there was a tender, quirky woman, striving to break out; the type of woman who would be an asset to any business. If Caz could only lose her big city pretensions and realise that money wasn't everything, she might even make a good job of Stone Break House. The house had never been intended to impress, it had been built as a home. He wanted her to understand that, to see things as they were. 'I'm not trying to humiliate you,' he assured her, holding her in front of him.

'You'd better not,' she warned him, holding his stare.

He kept his promise as the music overtook them. Holding her round the waist, he made sure she was travelling in the right direction. As soon as he was certain he changed his grip to her wrist to give her more freedom, but then he noticed how slender it was; fragile. He changed again to draping an arm across her shoulders. He decided to lead her to a part of the platform where she would be less exposed. Dancing with her felt good, even when their fingertips were barely touching; she felt good. He was more relieved than he could express. If she had retired into the shadows or had refused him and bolted it would have been a giant step back.

'Galem, I—'

'No…' He wouldn't allow any hesitation now. Dipping his head so he could stare her in the eyes, he placed a finger over her lips, stifling her complaint. No, he mouthed with a smile of encouragement.

'I'll break your toes…'

'I'm prepared to risk it.'

He proved it, swinging her into the air and carrying her as they danced so that her feet didn't touch the ground once. She glared into his eyes, pretending to be angry, but he could see she was enjoying herself. It made him smile. He didn't like pushovers in any area of his life; they were no use to him. He liked the idea of being a wall for Caz to kick against, especially when it made her lose her inhibitions and relax.

CHAPTER SIX

'IS THIS your idea of dancing, Galem?' Caz said as he whirled her round.

'It's the safest option,' he said with honesty.

She looked at him, undecided for a moment, and then her face broke into laughter. He laughed too. He felt as if he'd just cut the greatest deal of his life. After that she melted a little and then a little bit more. She was starting to trust him and feel safe, which made him feel good. They were having a good time; a great time. She could hold his gaze with confidence and laugh into his eyes. It was as if she'd crossed some huge divide and found it was fun on the other side.

When he set her down he steadied her with the greatest care, one hand on either arm. He was in no hurry to let her go, no hurry at all. He'd never felt like this before. They stood in silence for a moment staring at each other and then, and only because he felt it was too soon to move things on, he said, 'I promised you'd enjoy this, didn't I?'

SUSAN STEPHENS 75

As the musicians had sensed a change in mood
was called for the music slowed to a seductive
rhythm, and a plangent melody rang out. The urge to
draw her close overwhelmed him. He gave in to it.

This time it was easy, she melted in his arms, and
it was he who had to adjust his position. He didn't
want to frighten her, she felt so good, but the vul-
nerability he had sensed made him check the desire
to pull her as close as he wanted to. What he wanted
was to feather kisses all over her face, and run his
tongue down her neck to her cleavage and hear her
moan. He wanted to suck her ear lobe and rub his
stubble against the sensitive hollow above her collar
bone. He wanted to make love to her.

'Come here, come closer, townie…' He noticed
how she quivered when his warm breath brushed her
neck. He inhaled deeply, or maybe that was a sigh of
contentment; he made them so rarely, he hardly knew.

This was like nothing she'd ever experienced
before, Caz thought as Galem's arms closed around
her. A lifetime of no hugs and then these hugs from
this man. What was a girl supposed to do?

Galem was the first man, the first person to take
her in his arms and hold her close. She was deeply
affected by it, and perhaps in danger of reading too
much into it. She was glad to have the steady rhythm
of the music soothing her. If nothing else she had
this to bank, along with all the other things she'd felt
since meeting Galem.

He coaxed her to move gently with him until she

relaxed. First her shoulders and then her arms, and now one of her hands had crept up to rest alongside her face against his chest. Her other hand was enclosed in his, though that was different. She was frightened to move it, even a little bit in case of the wrong messages.

The wrong messages? She wasn't sure how much more she could afford to relax brushing intimate parts against him. She guessed a man like Galem would be used to more sophisticated lovers and would think nothing of it. He would expect her to be like all the rest, but she wasn't...

His hands tightened around her as if he sensed her anxiety. She had to stop thinking these thoughts. He could read her too easily.

Caz tried to persuade herself that she was over-reacting. She told herself firmly that this wasn't an earth-shattering moment, or even an occasion for examining all the stuff in her head—it was just a dance.

Just a dance?

Nothing so far had been that simple with Galem.

She straightened up and eased back, smiling up at him to show she was enjoying herself in the most platonic way. He brought her close again, nuzzling against her briefly in a gesture she was sure was meant to give her confidence. She consciously relaxed. She didn't want to make a scene, or have Galem thinking he was wasting his time trying to entertain a sulky woman who didn't know how to enjoy herself. This was just a bit of fun, and there was nothing wrong with that.

Caz was surprised to discover how well they fitted together even though he was so much bigger than she was. She couldn't help wondering if he found her attractive, and then told herself not to be so silly. Why would he? There were lots of pretty girls around, girls without issues, girls who loved the countryside as much as he did, and would slot into his life right away.

'Are you enjoying yourself yet?' He dipped his head to ask the question, staring into her eyes so she couldn't look away.

He had no idea how much. 'Yes,' she said, with a smile that was both genuine and guarded. She didn't want him to think she was making a play for him. She didn't want him second-guessing her thoughts either.

And then instead of looking away as she had expected he kept on staring at her. His eyes were warm and kind, and she had to stop staring at his lips. Kind. He was kind. Galem was just being kind to her.

She was like a feather in his arms, and the thought of matching his strength against her softness, of placing that strength at her disposal, was dangerously appealing. He knew more than anyone that just occasionally you had to give in to temptation. He made a signal towards the stage she couldn't see to keep the tempo of the music slow.

This time when he brought her close she came to him as if she belonged there. She was growing brave enough to tease him, testing herself against him before pulling away. He found that a real turn-on.

The rhythm of the music throbbed suggestively all around them; it reached up through the soles of their feet, making every part of him vibrate. He wondered if she felt as aroused as he did. He wondered about her inexperience. Did she have any experience of men at all?

He fixed his stare on the rapid pulse beating in her neck. She'd had fun and relaxed and had opened up to him. She had revealed herself to him in more ways than she knew. And he couldn't deny he was puzzled by what he'd learned. She was a woman in two parts, which only made the urge to know her better all the more tantalising and pressing.

As the song ended she tensed as if she was unsure what to do next. He held her lightly in a way that allowed her to break away should she want to do so, but she didn't move.

Caz hesitated as the lights dimmed still further, heralding the end of the evening. As the silence between songs lengthened she thought it the longest moment she had ever endured. She wasn't ready to stop dancing with Galem, but she was poised to pull away, to smile brightly and thank him—for the most erotic experience of her life, though, of course, she wouldn't tell him that.

As the music started up again Galem's hands

made her quiver as they moved slowly and confidently to draw her back; she sank against him,
stifling the urge to whimper with pleasure as he
traced the length of her spine with one firm hand.
He continued on again, moving up with his fingers
splayed until he reached her hair, and then, cupping
the back of her head, he began massaging her with
his thumb at a very sensitive place just below the
base of her skull. His other hand had found the sway
in the small of her back above her buttocks. She
arched towards him, she couldn't stop herself. Her
breath caught in her throat as she realised what she
was doing. It was a blatant invitation for him to
explore further.

A small shift of his fingers told her he'd got the
message. Her chest felt as if a band had been tightened around it, and very intimate parts of her were
growing so heavy. The sensation was new to her, and
it seemed to take her over. She had never done this
with anyone; she had barely acknowledged her sexu-
ality. Needs were for other people, not for her.

Was Galem aroused? Caz wondered. His gaze
was darkened. Was that a sign? When it transferred
to her lips she stared openly at his mouth. Then,
closing her eyes, she tried to imagine what it would
feel like to be kissed by him. The music must be to
blame, she realised, dragging herself back.

He watched all this, anticipating it and understanding it. He was in no hurry. He wanted Caz to
feel her need, to feel it growing, and he wanted the

pleasure of seeing it roll out until she couldn't hold onto it any longer. Every part of him was intensely aware of her, and of the hunger that was breeding inside them both. Lacing his big fingers through her tiny ones, he brought her hand to his lips and kissed it. She made a tiny moan deep in her throat and pressed against him. It was enough for now.

Their hearts were beating in unison and their limbs were as close as limbs could be. Each tiny space between them had disappeared one by one. With a sigh she angled herself, bringing his thigh between her legs. He could feel her warmth brushing against him, and his imagination filled in the sweet swollen spaces. Holding back like this was agony. He wanted to sweep her into his arms and carry her away and make love to her all night, all day, for as long as it took to feel sated.

He couldn't think of anything else, and she was making it impossible, resting her head against his shoulder, leaning into him, applying subtle pressure to his thigh, which she must think he was oblivious to. He helped her, just a little, just enough. He didn't want to frighten her or have her suspect what he was doing. Tiny thrusting movements answered him. She was desperate for firmer contact, but so was he. He loved to hear her sigh. He loved to dip his head and see the focus disappear from her eyes. He loved watching her, and he wanted to see more. He wanted to watch her in the throes of real pleasure, and he wanted to be the one bringing her that pleasure. And

above all that Galem thought, easing away, he wanted
to see wonder take the place of the wariness in Caz's
eyes.

'Bravo,' he whispered, when the music died
away. 'You're relaxed…'

Relaxed? This was full and total meltdown. 'I'm
a little hot,' Caz admitted. Hot? She was on fire,
inside, not out. She was suddenly aware of how far
things had gone.

Whispering in her ear, Galem suggested it was a
good time to take a break. The next moment her
heart was thundering with panic. She was suddenly
shy and bitterly aware of her own inexperience. She
had led him on, and now no doubt he expected…

They were halfway to the door when Galem
tipped his chin towards some hay bales where all the
other wallflowers were sitting out. It was a gesture
to suggest she join them.

Realisation swept over her in a hot cloud of humiliation. She should have guessed, he'd had
enough of her. There were still some dancers on the
floor, pretty girls…he probably wanted to partner
them. 'I'll be fine,' she said brightly as he excused
himself and walked away.

It was time for another reality check, Caz realised
as the minutes passed with no sign of Galem. There
were two possibilities, neither of which reassured
her. Either she had failed the test and he had dumped
her in favour of a go-faster model, or she had passed
with flying colours and he was visiting the men's

room to equip himself for whatever came next. And she still didn't have a bed for the night. She would wait here for a few more minutes, and then she'd start asking around. Someone had to know where she could stay, and if all else failed she still had a nice big bath to share with the mice.

But it wasn't in Caz's nature to sit around waiting for things to happen. There was nothing to be gained by dwelling on the fact that she was sure she had just made a complete and utter fool of herself with Galem. Her glance strayed to the door leading outside.

Once outside she was able to gain a little perspective, to remember who she was and why she was there. She was Caz Ryan, and she'd always survived whatever life threw at her. After a while standing outside in the night air proved a lot colder than she had imagined, and, hugging herself tight, she returned inside the hall.

'You have to join the line for food, love,' a helpful voice suggested.

The line snaked right round the hall, Caz noticed now, and she had seen enough of lines tonight to last her a lifetime.

'Too late—'

It wasn't just her heart this time but her whole body that gave a little leap at the sound of Galem's voice. For one crazy tilted second she felt like a teenager on her first date.

Cassandra would have been ashamed of her, Caz

thought. 'Too late for what? Another dance?' She kept it casual.

'Too late to join the line for food. It's all gone.'

'What?' Her face crumpled. Galem had no idea how hungry she was.

His cheek creased in his trademark smile, warming every part of her except her empty stomach. 'I'm afraid so. You'll have to be quicker off the mark next time, Cassandra.'

'Caz,' she reminded him. 'You can't mean it's all gone?' The scent of food was still heavy on the air. She refused to believe it until she saw the people in the kitchen pulling the shutters down. 'But that's not fair.' She turned to Galem as if he could do anything about it. 'We danced our hearts out. Haven't we paid our dues ten times over?' She was certain Galem had never worked so hard for a meal in his life.

'Lucky for you I had two put aside, isn't it?'

'You did?' Her face lit up and before she knew it she had thrown her arms around his neck. He felt so good it frightened her. She drew her arms back the moment she realised he'd made no attempt to reciprocate, quickly adapting her smile into something more prudent.

'That's where I've been,' Galem said, eyes burning with amusement as he tipped his chin towards the kitchen. 'I wanted to make sure you got something to eat—'

'And somewhere to stay,' she reminded him.

'That too,' Galem reassured her.

As he smiled at her she had to tell her arms to stay where they were and behave.

'Come on, townie. I'll sort you out.'

There was a distinct possibility she might let him, Caz realized, heart pounding as she followed Galem across the floor.

CHAPTER SEVEN

IT WAS agony standing waiting for their food to be dished up and Caz was practically dribbling by the time Galem had coaxed an extra portion of chips out of the plump lady in charge.

He found them a window sill outside in the hall where they could perch and balance their paper plates on their knees.

'So you found me somewhere to stay?' Caz prompted him as soon as the first few delicious mouthfuls had slipped down her throat.

'Somewhere I think you'll like,' Galem promised, forking up some food. 'Here, open your mouth.'

She stared at him blankly.

'Open,' he repeated.

She had plenty on her plate, but Galem wanted to feed her, and he was picking out the best bits for her.

'I guessed you'd like that,' he said when she'd finished.

She had. But it was the teasing tone of his voice that carried warmth all the way to her toes. 'This is all very—'

'What?' he interrupted.

His arm was brushing hers: warm, strong, hard.

'Casual? Nice? Or not posh enough for you, Cassandra?'

Caz drew back a little. Galem had a way of looking in her eyes as if he could read every secret she had. There was no point in bending the truth with him, anything less than a straight answer and he'd know immediately. 'It's nice,' she said. 'Very nice.'

Crazy but true. She was eating off a paper plate with a plastic fork in a village hall painted municipal magnolia, seated on a window ledge overlooking the dustbins, and it was wonderful. Normally she was allergic to anything that came within a mile of a deep-fat fryer, but tonight? Well, tonight was different in a lot of ways…for the first time in years she felt relaxed.

She looked up at Galem and couldn't believe the impact he had on her. Was it really only hours since her car had slipped into a ditch?

Galem's lips were really beautiful…

As Caz's mind continued to ask questions that her brain resolutely refused to answer Galem pointed to the pile of mushy peas on her plate.

'Don't you like them?' he said, forking some up and eating them.

'Not so much.' They held too many memories,

though she wouldn't tell him that. As a child growing up in a series of dreary institutions she'd often begged them from the fish and chip shop together with the chunks of batter that fell off fried fish. The small amount of money she had received as her allowance had invariably been directed towards, if not to the improvement of her diet, then at least to its diversity.

'Mint sauce,' Galem said, breaking into her thoughts, 'that's why they taste so good.' He murmured with pleasure as she accepted a mouthful from his fork. 'Didn't I promise you'd like them?' As he spoke he reached and brushed the hair from her face.

He took his hand away too soon, she wanted to feel his touch again, wanted it to linger this time, wanted to be alone with him, far away from here, from everyone, but...

Caz gazed down at her hands. She wasn't ready for this. She wasn't ready for Galem. Everything was moving too fast, and a man like him was for advanced students only, not novices like her.

He found more tasty morsels for her to eat, and finally she joined in, feeding him chips. It became a race to the finish, which ended in a very messy finale.

'Greedy townie, I ought to punish you for that.' Catching hold of her hand, he held her firmly so she couldn't feed him any more. The look he gave her sent her pulse rate soaring. If she was trying to be sensible she was going the wrong way about it. She was relieved when he had to turn away to take a call.

She tried not to listen, but it was hard not to when he was sitting next to her. He seemed to be talking about some big project and vast sums of money; that surprised her. 'Business on a Friday night?' she said curiously when he slipped the phone back in his pocket.

'Business twenty-four seven, I'm afraid.'

'Your employers must be very demanding.'

He missed a beat. 'Yes, they are.'

She guessed that talk like this must graze his ego, and so she dropped the subject, but it worried her to think she might have to pay a lot more for Galem's services than she had originally thought.

'Let me take that for you,' he said, piling her plate on his. 'Did you enjoy it?'

He had no idea how much. 'Delicious,' she said carefully. She watched him cross the room and dispose of their paper plates in the dustbin bag provided. It was strange to think of this powerhouse of a man being at the beck and call of anyone, let alone people who intruded on his Friday night. But if he loved Hawkshead and had a yen to own Stone Break House one day she could see how it might hold him back.

'We'd better go,' he said when he returned, glancing at the door. 'You still want a bed for the night, don't you?'

'You haven't told me where yet.' Her heart rate doubled.

'Come and see,' he said, holding out his hand. 'I think you're going to like it.'

She wanted to trust him, wanted to go with him, but whatever little common sense she had remaining kept on nagging at her—she didn't know him. On the other side of the argument she'd had a great night. For once she'd let go and become the person she really wanted to be. Plus just about everyone in the hall seemed to know Galem, seemed to like him too…

Okay, she had to make a decision. Like most big men Galem was growing restless; inactivity killed him. She needed somewhere to stay and by going with him it might help her achieve her original thought to employ him as a handyman for Stone Break House. If she went with him now it would give her the chance to find the best way to steal some of his time away from his present employers. Lots of people held down more than one job and were glad to do so, why should Galem be any different?

'You'll feel better after a nice hot shower…'

Caz realised she was frowning at him. But the thought of a nice hot shower certainly got through, especially when she remembered the bathroom at Stone Break House. What Galem was dangling in front of her was the prospect of heaven. 'A hot shower with a door?' A bathroom door had always been an obvious fixture until she'd seen the state of Stone Break House.

'The last time I looked there was a door.'

'With a lock?'

'Naturally.'

'And a window with a curtain I can draw?' Remembering Old Thomas, Caz thought it better to be sure.

'Two, but they have blinds, both working.'

Galem was waiting, but her mind was already made up. Her new home, Stone Break House, wasn't fit to live in yet, and she needed somewhere to rest her head for the night. 'Where is this place? And don't tell me it's a surprise.'

'My place…'

'Your—' Caz's voice stuck in her throat.

'Best I could do at short notice.'

His lips pressed down. Was that with regret or reluctance?

'Ready?' he said, glancing at the door.

As she nodded Caz took it as confirmation that she had finally gone mad. She was going to accept the invitation of a man she didn't know to take a shower at his place and spend the night there.

Her heart drummed a tattoo as she thought about it. Men like Galem were great to admire stripped to the waist on a building site, or in some cheeky advertisement, but she had never come this close to the real deal. Could she handle it? Galem was so big and so confident, while underneath her Bailey Brown shell she was still Caz Ryan from the children's home, still uncertain of herself and her place in the world.

People brushed by as she hesitated. Uncertainty crept in…

Snap out of it! Caz told herself impatiently. She'd made a good life for herself in London, and she could do it again in the north of England. She wasn't a weakling, she was a survivor, and she'd survive this night just like all the rest. 'I'm ready if you are,' she said.

'We're here,' Galem had stopped outside a smart-looking cottage, which formed part of a neatly kept terrace.

Caz's heart leapt as she viewed the newly painted front door and the clean step, but she had learned in life not to take anything for granted. 'Is this your place?'

'It's your bed for the night.'

It was perfect! She turned her face up to thank him, and got the same shock she always got when she looked at Galem. He affected her more deeply each time. His thick dark hair refused to be tamed and as he raked it back she longed to run her fingers through it. Caz stood transfixed as Galem put the key in the lock.

'Well, are you going to stand there all night?'

'This is fabulous,' she said, taking everything in as she walked inside. Fabulous? It was incredible. The cottage was nothing short of a miracle in Hawkshead. It was London chic in a charming Yorkshire shell, all stripped pine floors and cool cream interior, with terracotta throws and hand-knotted rugs. There was even a touch of black tinted glass and steel in the tiny kitchen to make her feel at home. 'I love it,' she said honestly, turning full circle. 'And your employers loan you this?'

'No.'

'So who owns the cottage?' She didn't mean to be rude but her thoughts just blurted out.

'I do,' Galem said as if it were no big deal.

'You?'

'Now, Cassandra,' he drawled disapprovingly, 'surely you of all people could never be accused of judging a book by its cover, could you?'

His voice rose at the end of the question as if he expected an answer. Had Cassandra's fame spread to Hawkshead? Something in Galem's eyes made a chill run through her. She was overreacting again. She was just telling herself to relax when she remembered her overnight bag.

'What's up?' Galem looked at her.

'I've got nothing with me. My bag—'

'Is already here. I put it upstairs in the bedroom.'

Bedroom singular? Was there only one? 'Look, Galem, I can't take your room.'

'Why not?'

'I don't know you.'

'I don't know you either,' he pointed out. His lips were starting to curve. 'Would I be safe?'

She met his gaze, raised a brow and chose not to answer.

'Shower?' he reminded her, shrugging off his jacket.

As Galem hung his jacket on a peg by the door Caz tried not to notice how powerful his shoulders were. Instead she made some fast calculations. There were two comfortable-looking sofas, and she could sleep on either one of them. A wood burner was chuckling happily away, so she would be warm, and the throws looked cosy. 'I'll take the sitting room you take the bedroom—how about that?'

'Shower first?' he suggested, sidestepping the question.

That made sense.

Galem opened the door on a small, neat bathroom that smelled as clean as if it had just been installed. Pointing to a cupboard, he said, 'And you'll find lots of clean towels in there.'

Bliss! She guessed this must be a guest bathroom as there were no personal items on show. The master bedroom had been created out of two smaller rooms, he had told her, and that had an *en suite*.

A smart terrace with two bathrooms? She was going to have to revise her budget if she wanted to entice Galem to work for her. Whatever type of building work he was involved in, it was certainly profitable. The cottage was like a luxury apartment, only far more spacious.

She would have to find the money to employ him from somewhere. Everywhere she looked in the cottage the workmanship was of the very best, and that was what she wanted for Stone Break House.

The proceeds from the sale of her London home had gone on the penthouse in Leeds—she hadn't been able to resist the views—and so she didn't have a lot of spare cash to play with, but the thought of abandoning the old house to its fate was out of the question. The setting in the quarry might look grim at first sight, but she had seen restoration projects where even ugly mining scars had been planted and softened. In the visual sense Stone Break House was a romantic ruin, but she was sensible enough to know that in practical terms there was a lot to do. And do it she would. Each time she thought about the old house she felt a tug. The project was on, and so was Galem. Somehow she had to find a way to afford both of them.

Caz waited until she could hear Galem banging about in the kitchen before stripping off her clothes. It excited her to be naked in his house while he was just a few feet away. Her nipples tightened as she turned on the shower; just the thought of employing him was addictive. By the time she switched off the shower Caz was doubly determined to sign him up. Bathrooms like this were exactly what she wanted at Stone Break House. She could have stood under the power shower all night...

She might have to, Caz discovered when she looked in vain for the towels Galem had promised she would find in the cupboard. She searched every inch of space before considering her options: she could jump up and down and shake herself dry, or she could stand dripping, naked, and yell for help.

When he heard her Galem chuckled. Knocking on the bathroom door, towel in hand, he added, 'My apologies…'

She had opened the door a crack to reach through it, and to his credit Galem kept his gaze fixed firmly on her face. It was inevitable that their hands would brush, and maybe because she was warm from the shower and naked fire shot to her elbows and all points beyond. Galem's hands felt wonderful: warm, dry and smooth.

Leaning against the door jamb, he glanced inside. 'Do you have everything you need?'

Caz glanced at the bundle of fluffy white towels Galem had just placed in her arms and then at him. 'No' rang in her head. 'Yes, thank you.'

'There's a robe hanging on the back of the door you can use.'

The thought of snuggling into a soft towelling robe seemed like bliss. She'd rinsed her underwear in the shower and was intending to risk commando again. A Galem-sized robe was as good as a tent. Perfect. No risk of exposure this time.

And she might as well douse that disappointment. She wasn't a wanton sex kitten, she was an inexperienced virgin with a problem on her hands. Galem earned a lot more than she'd thought, judging by the quality of everything at the cottage, so she

was facing some serious competition on the remu-
neration front. She would have a serious rethink
about his package.

Or not.

The Reader Service™ — Here's how it works:

NO STAMP
NEEDED!

THE READER SERVICE™
FREE BOOK OFFER
FREEPOST CN81
CROYDON
CR9 3WZ

NO STAMP
NECESSARY
IF POSTED IN
THE U.K. OR N.I.

CHAPTER EIGHT

AS SHE emerged from the bathroom Caz could hear Galem pottering about in the kitchen. As far as he was concerned her desirability factor score was zero. She should be grateful. If Galem had decided to turn up the heat she would have turned tail and run, and where would she sleep then? 'Without milk for me, please…' He was brewing fresh coffee in the kitchen.

The kitchen was small, but surprisingly well equipped. It was also extremely clean. Someone liked cooking, Caz gathered, gazing around. Galem continued to challenge every opinion the Cassandra in her had formed of him.

There was one problem with a small kitchen: space was at a premium with six feet four of solid muscle taking up most of it, which meant that she had to press back against the wall to let Galem pass. She tensed as his body brushed her lightly and hoped he hadn't noticed.

He carried the coffee through to the living room for them on a tray. She was still staring into space daydreaming about what it would be like to have a man like Galem want her. Having put the tray down he came back, squeezing past before she had chance to move.

'Sorry,' he said, reaching over her. 'I need the sugar. I'm guessing yours is without, right?'

Caz held her breath as Galem paused halfway across her. She felt as if she were wobbling on a tightrope with all sorts of forbidden pleasures lurking underneath. When the green eyes looked into hers she blurted the first thing that came into her head. 'Don't you know sugar's bad for you.?'

'They say that all the best things in life are bad for you.'

Caz closed her eyes briefly to absorb this, and when she opened them again it was to find Galem's lazy smile only inches from her mouth.

'But I can tell you with absolute certainty,' he said, murmuring the words so close to her lips they started tingling, 'that *they* are wrong. But maybe not about sugar,' he conceded with a shrug. 'So, I'll let you put it back in the cupboard for me, shall I?'

She was staring at his lips, Caz realised, quickly reorganising her eyeline.

'Sugar. Cupboard,' Galem prompted her. 'You've saved me from myself, Caz. Does that please you?'

If he moved maybe she could breathe again and answer him.

'I'll do it, shall I?' he said, moving past her.

As Galem put the sugar jar in the cupboard Caz's stomach turned over. She couldn't pretend she wasn't disappointed. If he had wanted to kiss her he'd had plenty of opportunity, so she could put that out of her head once and for all.

She hovered by the kitchen door as he settled down on the sofa. Having drained his mug, he put it down on the table, and, reaching forward, he started to unlace his boots. Kicking them off, he wriggled his toes and then, turning to her patted the seat next to him. 'So come here and tell me about yourself, Caz.'

She froze. 'Nothing to tell.' That was far too much man and far too little sofa.

'Nothing?' Galem's brows drew together as he stared at her. 'There must be something. You inherit Stone Break House from an aunt you've never met; you hold down an important post in the city. Fill in a few of the blanks for me, Caz. That's not asking too much, is it?'

It was a great deal too much to ask. She never discussed her private life with anyone—how could she when Cassandra lived one life and she lived another? How could she explain that to Galem? A man like him would never understand. He had probably lived in Hawkshead all his life and wouldn't understand the pressures. He wouldn't understand the need for Cassandra. 'I'm very boring,' she said. 'How about you?'

'Not boring at all,' Galem assured her. 'And I wouldn't describe you that way either…Cassandra.'

She didn't like the way he said the name, it made her nervous. 'Let's just say I'm a very private person,' she said, hoping he'd take the hint.

'That I can live with,' he said. 'Now, are you going to sit down, or are you going to stand there all night?'

If she wanted Galem to work for her she had to re-establish her credentials and fast. And lurking by the door as if he terrified her was not the way to do it. Caz clicked into business mode. 'Before I leave Hawkshead we must make an appointment to conduct a proper inspection of Stone Break House.'

Did she imagine it, or did he flinch at her use of the word 'must'? If his current employers were into coaxing perhaps she had better try it. 'I'd really appreciate your opinion,' she modified, 'and I promise not to take up too much of your time.'

'Tomorrow's Saturday,' he responded flatly.

She should have been on the point of nailing the deal, but instead she was floundering on the back foot like a novice. Patience, Caz instructed herself firmly. Had Cassandra ever failed to win a suitable candidate over rival companies? Leaving her mug in the kitchen, she went to perch next to him on the sofa. 'I realise it's Saturday tomorrow,' she said in a concerned voice, 'but I return to work on Monday—'

'And?' He frowned.

And she couldn't expect him to understand the demands of a high-powered job, Caz reminded herself. 'And so tomorrow is the only chance I have to sort out what we're going to do about Stone Break House—'

'We?'

'I thought you wanted to be involved?'

'You're jumping the gun, aren't you? I haven't agreed to anything, yet.'

Moistening her bottom lip, Caz looked up at Galem through her lashes. 'But you will…' She had everything crossed.

Lust roared up inside him, obliterating every rational thought he'd had about her since they'd met. She was sitting very close, and the look she'd just given him had made him hard. As she leaned towards him he could see the swell of her breasts beneath the neck of the robe. Pressing back against the sofa, he kept his distance, but that couldn't help him when her hand came to rest on his thigh. 'Caz—'

'Galem, I need you…'

His intention had been to remove her hand from his leg, and warn her that the sort of tactics she was employing could get her into a whole lot of trouble, but as his fist closed around her tiny hand she sighed. That was it. Instead of pushing her hand away he twined his fingers through hers. The ache in his groin had grown into a raging agony and inch by inch he drew her slowly towards him. 'Tell me to stop any time you want,' he begged her hoarsely.

'Don't stop,' she said breathlessly.

Her lips were rosy pink, the bottom lip full and slightly damp. Her top lip was beautifully etched in a perfect cupid's bow. Her eyes were slumberous, and her breathing was already rapid. The rise and fall of her chest drew his attention to the swell of her breasts beneath the robe. He wanted to part it and touch them, taste them, knead them, suck them, lave them with his tongue. It would only take the smallest move to close the distance between them and do that. Holding himself back was growing harder every minute and it was a glorious torment for a jaded palate.

Eyes closed, head back, she was offering herself to him. He feathered kisses on her throat to hear her whimper, and when she locked her fingers round his neck he kissed her lightly on the lips, brushing them, teasing them mercilessly. She was hot and sweet and eager, everything he had imagined she would be and more. She pressed into him hungrily, and the knowledge that she was naked beneath the towelling robe tormented him. Finally his hands found their way to her breasts. He could feel her nipples hard and extended even beneath the soft towelling fabric. He stroked them firmly with his thumbs on top of the robe while she clung to him, her eyes black with desire and her lips parted to drag in air. It pleased him to watch her pleasure unfold, just as he had always known it would. 'Do you like that?' he asked her roughly. 'Do you want more?'

Her answer was to lace her fingers through his and drag him close. The tender skin beneath her bottom lip had been abraded by his stubble and her lips were swollen from his kisses. He wanted her naked; he wanted to pleasure her in all the ways he knew how. He wanted to kiss her, nip her, taste her...

She dragged his shirt from the waistband of his jeans and placed her cool palms flat against his hard, warm, naked chest. It felt so good he gasped. Tugging off his shirt, he tossed it aside. She looked at him and he could read her mind. She wanted to feel his chest hair rasping her nipples against it. She wanted to feel his weight pressing down on her. She wanted him to part her thighs and ease the unbearable ache between her legs.

His hands moved swiftly to remove the belt on her robe. He tossed it aside impatiently. Opening the robe was like opening a very special gift. He kissed her again, pressing his hand against her belly and feeling her quiver. She couldn't keep still; her need was furious. She was beautiful, soft, round and rosy pink. As he dipped his head to tease her nipples with his tongue she strained against him, begging him not to stop, never to stop... He told her to be patient and she railed at him. His answer was to kiss her again, plundering the dark recesses of her mouth while she ground her body against him, on fire for him.

'I need you, Galem... I want you...'

He cupped her heavy breasts in his big hands, loving the weight of them and loving the engorged nipples that tempted him on. He suckled one and then the other while she encouraged him, calling out his name and making wordless sounds of need. She was showing him in every way she knew how much she wanted this. Her impatience drove her fingers cruelly into his naked shoulders, but whatever he did to her it wasn't enough—she wanted more.

'Do you want to make love?' he whispered against her mouth. 'Is that what you want, Caz?'

The need to feel her naked against him was overwhelming. He kissed her again, deeply, passionately, his hand tracking up her thigh, thrusting the towelling robe impatiently out of the way. She helped him in every way she could, writhing and thrusting against him as he kissed her neck and then her breasts. She was raking his back, exploring the hard muscles, and then she started fighting with the buckle on his belt. It came free in her hands and then the button fly yielded. She looked down, and, realising what she'd done, drew her hands away, leaving his jeans gaping. His erection was pressing hard against them; he was in agony. She made it worse, clinging to him, moaning, but some part of him still held back.

'Touch me,' she begged. 'Touch me there…'

He laughed softly against her mouth while his hands continued their exploration. 'You feel good,' he said, parting her lips gently.

'Do I?' she breathed.

'Oh, yes…warm, wet and very, very good…'

She was swollen and ready for him and as she exhaled raggedly he started stroking her more firmly. 'Is that what you want, baby?' he murmured, touching her rhythmically with just the tip of his finger.

She was keening softly, her hand pressed lightly over his. 'Yes, yes, do that, please…more…'

Little of what she said made sense, but it gave him a rush to see her in the throes of so much pleasure. She was ready for more and as he stroked her with his thumb he moved to go deeper, but as he did so she flinched and drew back. He knew right away.

'Why didn't you tell me?'

She sat up and hugged her knees to cover her nakedness, staring at him wordlessly with her big blue eyes.

'I'm not surprised you can't think of anything to say.' Reaching for his shirt, he put it on. He buttoned it up and tucked it into his jeans. Fastening those too, he secured his belt. Swooping down to pick up the discarded robe, he tossed it at her. 'Put that on.'

She looked at him sheepishly as she belted it. 'Galem, I'm—'

'Forget it, Caz. I'll sleep down here tonight. You take the bedroom.'

'I couldn't—'

He ignored her. 'There are clean sheets on the bed. And, Caz—'

'Yes?'

'Don't try that again with anyone. Ever. Under-stand?'

She paused without turning at the foot of the stairs. At least she had the good grace to blush.

'Good night, Galem…'

She could only see him in profile, and his jaw was set in an unforgiving line. He didn't answer; she didn't linger. Picking up the hem of the robe, she ran as fast as she could up the stairs and didn't stop until the bedroom door was firmly closed behind her.

Too humiliated to think, Caz dropped the robe, climbed into bed, and turned her face to the wall.

It was two o'clock in the morning. With a heavy sigh Galem put his wrist-watch back on the side table next to the sofa. His mind was in turmoil. He'd drifted off only to reach a half-world somewhere between sleep and waking, where Stone Break House had become more important to him than ever, and Caz was a virgin he could never touch. Would never touch again. The end result was a waking nightmare during which he tossed and turned, locked in an impossible quest to find a solution.

There were three burning questions going round and round in his head. Could he live with this level of frustration? Could he seduce a virgin? And what was going to happen when she found out who he was?

CHAPTER NINE

CAZ'S cheeks were still burning when she woke the next morning. She couldn't believe what had happened with Galem. Couldn't believe she had let things go so far.

Cassandra Bailey Brown and Galem going forward into the future was never going to happen and she needed her career. If Cassandra ever found a man it would be some rich city type. But without Galem to keep the project on stream there would be no Stonc Break House. The only thing she could do was to put her embarrassment to one side and pretend last night had never happened. She had to convince Galem that they could still work together.

Caz lay and listened to the silence, wondering if Galem was awake. If only things had been different, if only she had stayed away from him. There were good things in Hawkshead, though it made her smile to think of Cassandra accepting a future that included a crumbling ruin, a peeping Old Thomas, and a paver who liked throwing his weight around. But she had to think past Cassandra to a future when she could be herself. If she could be Caz Ryan in Hawkshead it would all have been worthwhile.

Having decided the best thing to do was take Galem a cup of tea and act naturally, Caz crept downstairs trying not to wake him. She made the tea and then took it into the living room where she could just make out his dark shape on the sofa beneath the throw. There was just enough light outside for her to draw the curtain a crack without putting the light on and disturbing him.

'Tea,' she whispered.

Throwing the covers back, Galem swung his legs over the side of the sofa, rubbed a hand across his eyes and stood up. He was completely naked. Retreating to the door, Caz hovered. 'Sorry, I didn't mean to. I mean, I—'

'You didn't mean to what?' Throwing himself down again, Galem held her gaze as he dragged the cover across his legs.

She mumbled something about tea and started backing out of the room.

'Caz, wait…'

'Shall I put it down here?' she said, skirting the sofa to put the mug of tea down on a side table. She was just straightening up when Galem caught hold of her wrist. She froze, but she didn't look at him.

'Caz, you can't brush this under the carpet.'

'Brush what…?' She kept on staring at the wooden floor, noticing how attractive the knots of wood were in the antique finish.

'What happened last night mustn't happen again.'

Galem released her wrist, but it took her a moment to react.

'I don't want to think of you putting yourself in danger like that,' he said. 'Not with anyone else. You mustn't risk it.'

There was a stinging sensation in her nose that always heralded tears. She straightened up and turned away. He was talking to her like a big brother.

'Promise me,' Galem said.

Silently, she nodded her head.

'Thank you for the tea.'

His voice was easy and relaxed—the old Galem. He was trying to make this easy for her, which perversely made it worse. She heard him put the mug down and reach for his wrist-watch.

'It's barely six o'clock in the morning, Caz.'

She turned round to see Galem raking his hair into some semblance of order.

'To what do I owe this honour?'

'I just thought we should make an early start.' She could see him curbing a smile.

'Well, you certainly did that.'

He flashed her a glance and scratched the stubble on his jaw, a stark reminder that parts of her were still burning from the rasp of it.

'I don't want to ruin your weekend, so I thought

we could start early on the tour round Stone Break House.'

'Good idea.' Sipping his tea, he sighed with approval, and then he gave her another of his penetrating glances, searching for anything more she might have on her mind.

'Would you work for me on a formal basis, Galem?'

'I already have a job.'

'I know that.' Buckling on her confidence, she went for broke. 'I also know you must be very good at it. You're obviously hugely appreciated by your employers, and I can see you wouldn't want to lose your position, but what I'm offering you is something you could do in your spare time.'

'I'm not sure I could work for a woman.'

She wasn't sure if he was joking or not.

'You see, I'm a traditionalist—'

'I would respect you absolutely. I wouldn't dream of throwing my weight around. I'd ask your advice every step of the way.'

When Galem winked she knew she'd been had, but would he take the job? Cassandra was always confident of the outcome of an interview, but she had messed up royally since coming to Hawkshead.

At least teasing her was an effective damper for his libido. He was relieved. After what had happened the previous night he was as keen as she was to get things back on an even keel. Even so, it was impossible to forget how she'd felt in his arms, hard to forget his sheer incredulity at discovering that anyone so sexually naïve could have survived intact for this long in the twenty-first century.

'I would pay you the fair rate, of course,' she went on thankfully, unaware of the track his mind was taking. 'And I'd be here every weekend, of course, pulling my weight…'

Pulling her weight? He had to hide his smile. She weighed around the same as a sack of feathers. But having concluded she must have swallowed a fistful of pride just to get to this point, he nodded sagely and let her go on.

'I'd like you to oversee the project and advise me. Team work, Galem,' she said, offering him the idea like the winning ticket in the lottery. 'Perhaps you could do some of the manual work for me too. We'll have a better idea when we go down there and take a proper look.'

She took it for granted that they would. Putting down his mug, he straightened up to face her. She didn't flinch; she squared her shoulders. He got a mental image of her in the boardroom: she'd be effective; she'd be good. 'I'm listening,' he said, reminding his eyes to curb the smile.

'My problem is time,' she explained. 'I've just taken on a new job, just moved up from London to Leeds, and I can't risk short-changing the work I do.'

'It means so much to you?'

'Yes, it does,' she said, honesty shining from her eyes. From her very beautiful eyes.

'So why Stone Break House?' he said, broaching the subject closest to his heart if not uppermost in his mind with Caz in the room. She was wearing faded pyjamas with teddy bears all over them. They trailed over her naked feet; her tiny naked feet. Clearly these were not one of Cassandra's designer purchases but something cosy she travelled with to feel safe in at night. She hadn't answered him he realised. They were staring at each other in a trance. He quickly snapped out of his. 'Why not choose an easier project than Stone Break House?'

'I never expect anything to be easy. And the amount of work ahead at Stone Break House doesn't frighten me.'

'There are plenty of beautiful conversions in the valley. You could sell Stone Break House and buy something smaller, but truly spectacular, with better views…' He had to try.

'No,' she said, firming her jaw. 'My mind's made up.'

He could see that.

'To be honest with you, Galem,' she went on without prompting, 'I can't even tell you why I want the house so badly. I just know I do. I don't think I ever met my aunt. There's no connection between us, or between me and Stone Break House, nothing that could explain how I feel about it—'

Her cheeks turned scarlet. She mashed her lips together, drawing his gaze.

'If you keep the house you'll need me to help you.'

'Yes, I will.' Hope sprang in her eyes as she looked at him. 'So will you help me, Galem?'

Better that than risk someone else interfering. 'You'd better go and get dressed,' he said, stirring. He saw her flinch and glance down to be sure the throw was still in place, covering him. Satisfied, she relaxed.

'Can't you see it, Galem?' she said as she was on the point of leaving the room. 'Can't you see Stone Break House when it's finished?'

He'd always been able to see it, but what interested him now was the way Caz's face changed as her imagination coloured in the spaces. Her expression was euphoric, and she looked truly beautiful. For a moment he bought into her dream, but then he reminded himself that Stone Break House was his home, always had been, and always would be.

'Well?' she said, prompting him. 'Will you help me?'

'What's in it for me?' Galem the paver had returned.

'Tell me if you can do it first,' she countered, showing him a glimpse of the businesswoman she would be during the week. 'Project management would look good on your CV,' she coaxed, her eyes burning into him.

'On my CV?' He tried not to laugh; this really wasn't the moment. He could practically see the cogs in her mind whirring, telling her that she'd made a blunder, and that men like him didn't have CVs.

'It would be good experience for you,' she modified quickly.

She could think on her feet and her professionalism wasn't in question. 'And do you think I need more experience?' he said, wrinkling his brow as if her opinion really mattered to him.

But she saw through that and her cheeks flamed red again. She blushed so easily it was wrong of him to tease her, but irresistible all the same. He could feel her willing him to break eye contact now, and so he held it a little longer. 'I tell you what I'll do,' he said at last.

'Yes?' She sat forward.

'I'll come to look over the house with you now, and we'll make a plan.'

'You will?' She wanted to go to him and throw her arms around him, tell him how much this meant to her, but, of course, there was no way she could do that now. Just to clear the air completely she said, 'This is strictly a business proposition, Galem.'

'I'm always open to propositions…'

Cocking his head to one side, he looked at her quite seriously, but then slowly the look in his eyes changed and he smiled his long, lazy smile that fired up every part of her. But she could sense the microscopic changes in his eyes that told of something hardening inside him; resolve, she guessed. He wanted the house as much as she did; she must never forget that. She knew that Galem resented the fact that she had inherited it, that anyone had inherited it. He thought Stone Break House should belong to him. As he looked at her now she was struck, both by the beauty of his eyes, and by the calculation in them. It suited him to indulge her for now, but eventually he would find a way to take the house from her.

The thought of an enemy as attractive and potentially dangerous as Galem clutched her innards and made them play circus games that involved lots of spinning and clenching. It couldn't be helped. For now he was the best chance she had. 'I'd like you to think about co-ordinating the project for me.'

'You don't know anything about me, or my abilities.'

True. Cassandra wouldn't have taken such a chance. Rasping a thumb pad across his jaw, Galem gave another of his cool, assessing glances.

Who was assessing whom here? She had never come up against anyone like this before. Lucky for her Galem was a one-off.

Caz's hand crept unconsciously to the tender spot below her lips where Galem's beard had abraded her. She felt a tingle of delicious dread at the thought of working with him on a regular basis, but never coming close to him again. 'We can soon put that right. You can tell me all about yourself as we go round the house.'

'You don't give up, do you?'

'Never.' She held his gaze. Galem's was pure irony. Had he never been through an interview process before? She guessed not. In his line of business recommendations would take him from job to job. 'It would just be a casual chat,' she reassured him.

He remained impassive.

'I'm more interested in you telling me what you think about the house.' She was trying to shift the emphasis so he'd feel he was on familiar ground.

His silence was unnerving.

'So there's no way you'd sell the house,' he said at last.

'Put that out of your mind, Galem. It's not going to happen. I'm going to restore Stone Break House with or without your help. If you agree to help I should warn you I'm short of funds right now, but I'd be able to take you for more hours quite soon.'

He held up his hand to stop her. 'Don't worry about money now, I'll think of a way you can repay me.'

Her body responded immediately, but her head intervened. Galem was always teasing her, or lecturing her; he didn't mean anything by it. The glint in his eyes still ran a quiver of awareness down her spine. She had to remind herself that Galem was simply telling her that she could keep the house just so long as that suited him, and not a moment longer.

But it didn't matter what his terms were, Caz realised, because the die was cast and she couldn't turn back now.

CHAPTER TEN

CAZ elected to walk to Stone Break House with Galem. She wasn't in the mood to be cooped up with him in a rusty Land Rover, or beat-up tractor. There was no pressure to talk to each other while they were walking in spaces that were vast, beneath a sky that was huge.

The early morning air was bracing, not cold, and even the hills didn't seem quite so daunting. Galem had been okay so far, quiet but relaxed, but as they approached the rusty gates his mood changed again.

His jaw set as his hand closed on the rusty gate latch. 'That lawyer really did spin you a yarn.'

'Perhaps.' She said it in a way that didn't encourage any more conversation on the subject. She could be just as stubborn, and use just as much imagery. She ran her fingertips possessively along the sunken railings, telling Galem without words to get over it and get it through his head that the house was hers and was going to stay that way.

As he pushed the gate open he said, 'It's a disaster,' as if that was an end of it, the end of the tour too, even before they set foot inside.

'I prefer to think of it as a blessing in disguise for both me and Stone Break House.' She strode ahead of him down the path.

He caught up with her at the foot of the steps, stopping her there. 'Meaning?'

'The house has been neglected and needs some love, and I need to get out of the office—'

'Job too much for you, Cassandra?'

Galem's question, plus the speed of it, startled her. 'Of course not,' she said, quickly refocusing. 'I like a challenge.' He started off round the back, and now she had to run to keep up with him. 'My legs are shorter than yours, in case you hadn't noticed.'

Noticed? He had conducted a full inventory, not once, but several times, and last night he'd almost completed his inspection. Sexually she was corked like a bottle of champagne waiting for the stopper to be removed, which puzzled him. She was a beautiful woman—not in the conventional sense, she was too quirky for that, but he liked quirky. So why was she so inexperienced?

He slowed to match her pace as they walked round. They had to find a way to get along. It was better he had a hand in the renovations from the start.

As they crested the hill and she saw the lights of the village down below them she turned to smile at him. 'It looks welcoming, doesn't it?'

It gave him a jolt to realise she was settling in, at least in her mind. But something inside him glowed. She was such a mix of stubbornness, assertiveness and eagerness. Just the sort of person you would want working for you…

'Do your employers live close by?' she said, distracting him.

That was one question he was never going to answer. 'Roundabouts…'

Why could she never get a straight answer from Galem? She was the one with a past to hide. What was wrong with him?

Country manners, Caz concluded. People were more reserved in Hawkshead. They liked to look at you and weigh you up before committing themselves to a conversation, and Galem was no different. But she had to find out something about him. Her plan could fail before she launched it if his employers felt they were entitled to Galem's services every waking moment. 'Do they give you plenty of time off?'

'Enough.'

Perhaps he worked in isolation and monosyllables went with the territory. She would just have to rein back her impatience for now. He would surely have a few hours to spare for her each week.

The dilapidation they found was worse than she had expected; it looked a lot worse in daylight. Caz's heart sank as they walked round together. It was a sad old house, not even close to being habitable. It would take more than money, it would take a miracle to make it right.

'Structurally, it's sound enough, though it needs a proper inspection by a building surveyor,' Galem told her as they continued their rounds.

'What about the roof?' She bumped into him, then hastily drew back, staring up to avoid looking at him. Any form of physical contact, even accidental, had to be avoided at all costs if she was going to pull this off. Employing Galem, not making love to him, was the future.

'I'd need to get up there to be sure.'

He brushed up beside her to take a closer look and she wasn't sure whether she'd give more away by moving or staying still. She opted for a return to the interview. 'Have you handled anything of this magnitude before, Galem?' She stood back to give him space.

'Similar things,' he said vaguely. 'If you'd like to check the quality of my work I could give you some addresses.'

'That would be great. Thank you. It's not that I don't believe you...' She forgot what she was going to say as Galem turned to look down at her. Prolonged eye contact like this was almost as bad as touching him. 'Bank managers always want proof,' she blurted, ripping off a chunk of plaster and with it half a wall.

'Hey, steady on,' Galem exclaimed, grabbing

hold of her arm. 'Damp has made this wall unstable. You don't want to start doing that.'

I really don't, Caz agreed with him silently, his warm hands coming into contact with her body as he started brushing the debris from her clothes.

'Let's go through to the kitchen,' he suggested. 'I'm thinking we could take this wall away without impacting on any of the original features.'

'You seem to know your way around pretty well?'

'I climbed in through a window. Your aunt's lawyer kept things locked up pretty tight.'

He didn't just want it for himself, he'd been making plans to restore it for some time, Caz thought as she watched Galem moving around. And he was right about taking the wall down. The large open-plan space that would create would make a fabulous family kitchen.

'Be careful! Don't tread there… Too late,' Galem murmured, catching her in his arms as a floorboard gave way and she lurched towards him.

She froze in his arms, not daring to move a muscle. Her heart was pounding so loud, surely he must hear it? His arms were so strong and he smelled so good; all of it, all of him reminding her… Reminding Her To Turn Her Face Away. But she couldn't. She just couldn't. She closed her eyes, melting…

'You follow me in future,' Galem said, setting her back on her feet again. 'You follow exactly in my footsteps, and you will not wander off. If you don't do as I say you'll have to wait for me outside. Do you understand?'

Her jaw worked. Her eyes filled. Who did he think he was talking to? But he was right, Caz conceded. Some parts of the house were more unsafe than others, and Galem had already been round. She firmed her mouth and nodded briefly. 'Bottom line, can it be saved?'

'Definitely,' Galem said with the air of a man who had already come to that decision.

She should be glad he shared her belief. They both felt Stone Break House was worth saving; didn't that endorse her decision to keep it? Their individual reasons for doing so were irrelevant. 'So, we have a deal?'

'I don't know, Cassandra... Do we?'

The tip of her tongue crept out, testing the redness beneath her lips. Could she work with him, or was she kidding herself? What if he had a girlfriend? What if he brought her here? How would she feel then?

Caz knew how she felt. Galem's fabulous eyes and wicked smile hadn't been wasted on a man who wasn't interested in women, and she doubted she could stand by each week and watch him walk away with someone else after they'd been working on the house together.

Unconsciously her gaze slipped to his lean hips, skirting past the well-worn fabric on his bulging

button fly. She couldn't have him, but if she even suspected anyone else of taking an interest in her project
manager she'd be hard pressed not to scratch their
eyes out.

'Something on your mind, Caz?'

'No. Why?' She had to calm down, and ease
back. Acting defensive was not the way forward.

Galem let it go. Easing his shoulders in a shrug,
he suggested, 'Shall we continue our inspection?'

They carried on, the tension sizzling between
them, until finally he said, 'That's enough for today.
I've got another appointment.'

What he said gave her a jolt, but after the way her
thoughts had been turning she should have known.
'Okay,' she said lightly. 'Where are you going?'
None of her business, but it slipped out before she
could stop herself.

'The dogs.'

'The dogs?'

'Greyhound racing. You can come with me if
you like.'

She was relieved by what he'd told her and by the
way his face creased in the familiar grin. Maybe they
could get on. Maybe this was a test. Galem was
offering her a real taste of northern life. Rough and
ready, casual fun, something Cassandra would have
loathed.

'Just remember,' he said, planting his legs and
folding his arms, 'I don't do waiting.'

'And I don't do tag along.' She had to be sure. Her

head was still full of the high-kicking glamour girls at the village hall who'd been drooling over him.

'I'm on my own, Caz.'

'Do you want me to say ah-h-h?' It was her turn to grin. She felt like saying a lot more than ah, she felt like cheering. Couldn't be helped that he saw how pleased she was to hear that.

'Well, are you coming with me, or not?'

She had to keep him on board, but after last night it was dangerous to show too much enthusiasm. 'Thank you for inviting me. I'd like that,' she said primly.

Galem scratched the side of his face and looked her up and down. 'Don't you have anything else to wear?'

So he'd noticed the cashmere suit was ruined? Right now it was all she had. 'I'm stuck with this,' she said, brushing her hands down the matted wool. 'It's seen one too many puddles, I guess, but I don't think my business suit would be appropriate.'

Galem's look told her she was right.

'No problem,' he said, moving towards the door. 'We'll go back to the cottage, pick up the Land Rover, and then I'll take you shopping.'

Her mouth fell open. 'You'll…' She was speechless.

'Do you have a problem with that?'

'No… No problem at all. Are you sure you don't mind?' Her heart was already lifting at the thought of shopping.

'It would be my pleasure.'

There was a glint in Galem's eyes that should have made her suspicious, but any man who took a girl shopping had to be a paragon of all the virtues. Didn't he? Caz thought as Galem quietly shut the door.

'Wash-and-wear trousers in Sherwood Green and a nice bright yellow shirt…'

Caz could only stand and wait for the shop assistant to ring her purchases through the till. Galem was standing guard at her back, preventing her from fleeing the shop. This was the best ladies *fashion* shop in Cleckhampton, he had assured her. And now she had to try not to notice how much he was enjoying this.

'A royal blue zip-up jacket…comfort-fit brogues *and* cushion-heeled socks. My, you'll be comfortable in that lot,' the sales assistant assured Caz, her rosy cheeks glowing pink with approval as she handed the bundle over the counter.

'I'll pay for them,' Galem said, pushing Caz's hand with its precious piece of well-worn plastic aside.

'No,' Caz protested hotly, but then he pointed to a sign: 'cash only'. 'I see,' she said, cheeks reddening. She hardly ever carried cash. 'Thank you,' she said meekly, vowing never to be caught out again.

'The changing room's over there,' the assistant said, pointing. 'And when you've finished I'll put your emergency outfit in a nice paper bag for you to take home…'

Home… The mere mention of it brought Cassandra back full force, forcing Caz to take a back seat. The contrasts were too stark to sustain her through an ordeal like this. Home was London or Leeds, both of which were blessed with one of the finest fashion stores in the world. Home was black, tan, beige and winter white, with the occasional shot of pewter grey. Home was not green and yellow and royal blue, with extra-wide comfort brogues and stay-high, cushion-heeled socks. Home was trophy carrier bags, design statements in themselves; home was not a paper bag.

'Happy now?' Galem said brightly as they climbed back into his beat-up Land Rover.

Ecstatic! Though she had the good grace to thank him for stopping off at the shop. Worst of all he looked great. He always did. Galem would have fitted just as well on Sloane Street as in Clackhandle, or wherever the heck they were.

She almost lost it when his warm hand briefly covered hers.

'Stop wringing your hands, Caz. You're sorted now.'

Sorted? She almost laughed out loud. She was about as far from sorted, as… She stared at her hand. Emotion washed over her. She could feel the imprint of each of Galem's fingers burning into her. Something to hold onto, she guessed.

He stopped in front of an unpromising pebble-dashed entrance. The building was single-storey and rambling and streams of people were already making their way inside. It was impossible to see anything beyond the high walls marking the perimeter.

'Security,' Galem explained. 'The race track is on the other side of that fence. You don't want anyone climbing over.'

'Where to now?'

'I'm meeting Old Thomas in the paddock. He's got my dogs.'

'Your dogs? You race greyhounds?'

'It's a team effort with Thomas.' He switched off the engine. 'He used to race with my father and now I've taken his place.'

It was the most he'd ever told her, Caz realised.

'Are you ready?' Galem said, leaning across to open the door for her.

The brush of his arm, the faint tang of his shampoo and his warmth enveloped her, forcing her to drag in a huge draught of fresh air as he opened the door.

'I bet you're glad you've got a jacket now,' Galem said as they got out.

It was nippy, but she'd have preferred the shelter of his arms to a serviceable jacket, Caz thought, zipping it up.

'Come on,' he said, finding her hand as if she were his kid sister. 'I'm going to take you to meet my babies.'

He drew her along behind him while she told herself not to get excited, and that the only reason he was holding her hand was because the place was packed and he didn't want to lose her. The way he talked about his dogs, his *babies,* that threw her a bit. Reining in feelings wasn't so easy when Galem could be so nice.

Caz's heart turned over while she watched Galem hunker down with his animals. The greyhounds clearly adored him, and were doing their best to lick the stubble off his face.

'They're gorgeous. Can I stroke them?'

'Of course you can.' He turned his face up to look at her. 'Do you like dogs?'

'I love all animals.' She didn't care if he thought she was trying to win him round. She had always wanted a dog, but her life had never allowed for one. As he rumpled their ears she said, 'I can see they mean a lot to you.'

'I love them,' he said simply. 'Thomas and I both do. They've got a home for life with us.'

Weren't dogs supposed to be good judges of character? Caz thought wryly as she watched the two greyhounds continuing to make a fuss of Galem. 'What are they called?'

'This is Hawkshead Sally,' Galem said as he stroked the smooth head of an intelligent brindle, 'and this black beauty is our champion, Stone Break Sid.'

Named after the house! 'Named after the house?'

Galem was so busy with his dogs he didn't appear to hear her. 'I'll just put their muzzles on before we take them in. You'd like to see them race, wouldn't you?'

Both dogs wagged their tails appreciatively as she patted them. 'Of course I would.' Who could resist those keen, bright eyes? And that was just the brown ones.

Galem handed the dogs over to their handlers for the meet, and then took Caz trackside to a prime spot alongside the winning post. It was an important race, he explained, in which Sid was up against some stiff competition. Galem stood behind her as the stadium filled up, keeping one arm either side of her body to protect her, trapping her between him and the rail. Having him so close was distracting and it wasn't until she saw the parade of dogs approaching Caz could think of much besides the warmth of Galem's breath brushing the back of her neck. It had raised each tiny hair and made every part of her tingle.

'I don't see Sally?' she said, turning to him with concern.

'Sally's an expectant mother, so she's not running today.'

'She's having puppies?' Caz's face relaxed into a smile. 'So why did you bring her?'

'Because Sid won't race without her. Look,' Galem said, leaning forward.

Caz snatched a breath as the sleeve of his shirt brushed her face. She could feel his warmth, and his legs were pressed into the back of hers. Her heart was racing so fast she could barely concentrate on what Galem was pointing out to her.

'The first dog in the line,' he prompted.

'Sid,' she said excitedly, transferring her attention.

'You can tell Sid's looking for Sally.'

It was true, Caz thought, looking at Galem. She knew how Sid felt. Leading the parade, Sid was definitely straining his leash looking for his mate. Galem's cheek was so close to hers she could feel the heat coming off him. And he was so pleased to see his dogs it was only natural he should drape an arm over her shoulder to point her in the right direction. Gradually she relaxed and started sharing his pleasure.

'Sid will run this race for Sally, and he'll win,' Galem predicted.

The idea of one dog depending on another made Caz smile. The fact that Galem believed it made her all warm inside, or maybe that was because Galem had been forced against her again by the weight of the crowd.

'Excited?' he whispered in her ear as the dogs were loaded into their racing traps.

'Extremely,' she said honestly, glad he couldn't see her face. The place was so packed they didn't have any option other than to be cuddled up close together. It was a relief when he started telling her about the race and what to expect.

It would be over in seconds, Galem explained. He

pointed out Sid's most likely challengers, and moments after that the electronic hare was released. It whipped in front of them at incredible speed, and then the trap doors sprang open. With a dip of their sleek heads the greyhounds broke for freedom in a pack. Caz had to rely on Galem giving her a commentary because to her inexperienced eye the racing dogs were a blur. Hearing Sid was in the lead, she jumped up and down, screaming with excitement, and when the dogs streaked past a second time she saw one black muzzle nudging ahead of the rest. 'Sid won!' Ecstatic, she threw her arms around Galem's neck.

'Yes, he did.'

Galem was staring down at her without making the slightest attempt to draw her close, Caz realised; if anything he had stiffened.

She slowly unlatched her fingers and stood back. 'Can we go and see them?' She was all hot and cold inside and feeling awkward again.

'I have to go and collect the prize,' Galem reminded her. 'You'll be coming with me, won't you?'

He never made it easy.

CHAPTER ELEVEN

IN THE winner's enclosure Stone Break Sid was looking as pleased as Caz guessed a dog could look, and at his side his sweetheart, the pregnant greyhound Sally, looked on adoringly. The dogs' history seemed to be tied in to Galem's, and that was perhaps the only clue she was going to get about him.

One clue was better than nothing, and she was determined to make the most of it. 'Did Sally ever race?'

Galem had just collected Sid's trophy and a cheque. He gave them to her while he took the leads to lead the two dogs away. 'Sally loved racing, but she always came last.'

'Was that a problem for you?'

'Never. Sid can't live without her, and, even if he could, Sally enjoys running. I wouldn't dream of stopping her while that's the case. When she isn't expecting she takes part in some racing I organised to give older and slower dogs a chance of glory.'

The more she learned about him, the harder it became to keep Galem in the pigeon-hole marked impersonal. She was touched by this new caring side of him, but she had also learned that he sponsored racing, which cost money. A lot of money. Before she could probe any further he said, 'Come on. Let's get out of here.'

Crowds were streaming past them in readiness for the next race, and they were being jostled. To protect her Galem held the leashes in one hand and steered a safe path for her with the other. Old Thomas was waiting for them in the car park, and he insisted on taking the dogs back with him. He made the comment that Galem should relax while he could.

He must work every hour under the sun, Caz concluded. He must do to be able to afford such a lovely house as well as keep racing dogs.

'Hungry?' he said, distracting her.

'Starving,' Caz admitted. Since arriving in Hawkshead her appetite had quadrupled.

They ate in the Land Rover outside a fish and chip shop, using plastic forks, and glugging everything down with a can of cola.

Something Cassandra would never do, Caz reflected as Galem disposed of their rubbish, but Cassandra wouldn't be here in the first place.

Swinging back into the driver's seat, Galem threw her a glance. 'Better now?'

'Much.' She held his gaze momentarily. It was the

best time she'd had for ages. She'd really enjoyed his company, and she had no doubt that if they'd been a real couple the date wouldn't have been close to reaching its end.

Forget that thought, Caz told herself firmly as a sheet of lightning lit up the cab. She wasn't Galem's type and this wasn't going anywhere, and now it was time for her to get on with her life.

But getting on with her life had to wait because when they returned to the cottage they found the storm had brought a tree down across the door. Several neighbours were out on the street, sheltering under umbrellas. As soon as they saw Galem they clustered round him as he got out of the car.

It had only just happened, apparently, and the general suggestion was to call the fire brigade.

'No need, I'll get the tractor,' he said, taking charge. 'You stay here,' he instructed Caz. 'I need to make sure the cottage is safe before you go in there.'

'Be careful…' He was gone before she could stop him, and she could only watch anxiously as he climbed over the branches and disappeared inside the house.

A tense five minutes passed when an ear-splitting crack made Caz cry out with alarm. The giant trunk had shifted and become more firmly lodged. Like many houses in the village the cottage backed onto another, which meant the front door through which Galem had entered was the only way out. The windows were old-fashioned and tiny—another example, no doubt of Galem's thoughts on keeping the essence of a house intact, but this time it would work against him. He would never be able to fit his shoulders through them.

Right on cue Galem's head poked out of the window as he tried to assess the situation.

'What can I do to help?' she yelled, coming as close as she could.

'Not much.' Galem scratched his chin and sighed.

'Call the fire brigade, mate,' someone yelled.

Galem squashed that one right away. 'They'll have enough to do tonight. This isn't an emergency.'

'Why don't I get the tractor?' Caz suggested. 'You can tell me what to do,' she insisted, determined to ignore the expression on Galem's face.

'Don't be ridiculous—'

'Why can't I drive the tractor?'

'Because you can't even drive a car!' he pointed out with a certain amount of logic. 'Plus you'd have to attach a rope—'

'Would I have to tie a knot too?' she said, growing angry.

She knew this was the worst kind of torture for him. Galem was used to being in charge, instead of which he was imprisoned. 'Just tell me what to do—where I can find ropes, how to start.'

'Absolutely not.' His voice was adamant.

'So what do you suggest?' Caz demanded, squaring up to him. 'Shall I start whittling?'

'Maybe we should call the fire brigade...'

She could see him reaching for his mobile phone, and called out, exasperated, 'This is hardly a life-threatening situation. It's something I can deal with, if you'll let me.'

Snapping his phone shut, he tried again to force his shoulders through the open window.

Caz pressed her advantage. 'I've had my accident for this weekend. Now are you going to trust me, or are you going to sit there and wait for men with better things to do to come and rescue you?'

That got a reaction. She could feel his indignation lashing her harder than the rain.

'Driving a tractor isn't like driving a car,' he said after a tense silence. 'And the tractor I've been using here in Hawkshead is ancient—'

'Is that the one that tipped me into a ditch? The one parked round the back of Stone Break House?'

'I was moving some rubble. And I didn't tip you into a ditch. You managed that very well all by yourself.'

So, her driving was hopeless—it could only get better. 'I don't care what you were doing,' she said, overlooking the fact that the renovations on Stone Break House had already started as far as Galem was concerned—and probably before she'd even arrived in Hawkshead. 'I'm well acquainted with your tractor,' she told him pointedly, 'so I know how old it is. I presume it dates from the time when men were men and women did as they were told?'

She had to admit it was a relief to hear him laugh.

'Can you use a gear shift?' he said, turning serious again.

'Of course,' she lied. How hard could it be? 'Where are the keys?'

'Here,' he said reluctantly, dragging them out of his pocket.

'Thank you,' she said as he tossed them down to her. 'And the keys to the Land Rover?'

Caz listened carefully as Galem gave her instructions on what to do when she drove the tractor and where to find the ropes she would need. 'I'll be back as soon as I can,' she promised, ignoring his sceptical hum.

'Half an hour and then I'm calling the emergency services.'

'You do that,' she told him, stalking away.

Caz's over-confidence was short-lived. Galem was right about the tractor. It was ponderous and unpredictable, with a wobbly gear lever as long as a walking stick. Just getting it started up was an achievement. The mud-caked pedals were each the size of a small paving slab and about as heavy to press down. Adjusting the seat wasted more precious time and even then she had to half stand to stamp the clutch into submission. Several false starts later she had managed to lurch forward an inch. Gritting her teeth in fierce concentration, she gripped the wheel firmly and stamped her foot down on the accelerator pedal.

'Slow down, slow down,' Caz cautioned herself grimly, arms spread wide on the huge metal steering wheel. Galem had warned her about the dangers of turning tractors over and she was rigid with fear. But she had done everything he had told her to do. The ropes they would need to lift the tree trunk away from the door were coiled at her side. But even with all Galem's instructions the thing that helped her most was the fact that she was as stubborn as she was scared. No way was she going to admit defeat.

There were ditches beckoning on either side and with the heavy rain and faltering headlights there was a real risk she might land up back where she had started on Friday night, and this time there would be no Galem to rescue her. So she would just have to travel at the speed of a slug, Caz concluded.

Galem was watching out for her when she arrived, straining his head out of the narrow window space. 'I didn't think you'd make it,' he admitted, grinning at her. 'And when you did, I wasn't sure you were going to stop.'

'Behave, or you can stay there,' she warned him, leaning out of the cab.

With Galem yelling instructions and an avid audience at every window in the street Caz managed to secure the rope. Climbing back on board, she revved the powerful engine and inch by inch dragged the tree trunk away. She pulled it to some waste land where it could be dealt with later, and then, switching off the engine, slumped back in her seat.

'You did good, Caz…' Wind and rain blew into the cab with Galem. Throwing the door back, he lifted her out. Or rather she tumbled into his arms, trembling all over.

'You did really good,' he soothed her as he carried her back to the cottage in his arms. 'You deserve a reward…'

A really big one, she hoped, gazing up at him.

'Brandy and milk?' Caz stared at the mug Galem had just pressed into her hands. He had sat her down on the sofa on top of a towel in the living room while he went to make the drink.

'With sugar,' he said apologetically. 'I know it's bad for you, but even bad can be good for you sometimes.'

She took a long look at him.

'Shock, for example,' he said, glancing away, 'needs sugar. So you have to make an exception this one time.' Wrapping her fingers around the mug, he insisted, 'Drink. You're wet through.'

'So are you,' Caz observed, slanting him a glance.

'But you've had one hell of an ordeal.' Galem couldn't help but be proud of her. Caz Ryan was beginning to get under his skin and he wasn't sure how much longer he would be able to resist her.

'Only one?' She smiled over the rim of the mug.

'You'd better get out of those wet clothes now,' he said. 'Strip. You can't sit there, dripping all over my nice clean floor.'

As soon as she got up and started peeling off her clothes he knew he'd made a mistake. He couldn't handle this much torment. Her figure was stunning, mouth-watering. Gym-toned and clad in what he could imagine was this season's lingerie—pale green with pink rosebud trim. He swallowed and turned away, trying to avoid her gaze.

Thrusting some towels in her hand, he pointed up the stairs to the bathroom. 'Strip off the rest of your clothes there. I'll stick them in the washer with mine.'

But it was too late—he'd caught the look in her eyes. He ran his gaze up and down her gorgeous body once again.

He had to get her out of his sight or he wouldn't be responsible for his actions. 'The hot water won't last for ever.'

Just as she'd thought, Galem wasn't interested. She'd proved herself with the tractor; she still felt the exhilaration. She wanted him to share that with her.

Brushing past him as seductively as she knew how, she walked up to the bathroom and shut the door. Turning the shower on full blast, she stood motionless for a second, catching her breath and trying to blank her mind to what she so desperately wanted, needed. If only he wanted her.

Once she was calm enough she stepped beneath the steaming spray. Turning her face up, she luxuriated in heat and daydreams in which she had turned into Superwoman. It had been a lot better than being Cassandra, because she had got to save the hero, whereas Cassandra was always more interested in squashing them. And where heroes were concerned, Galem came top of the list. Fully clothed, he looked amazing. She could only imagine how good he would look naked. Caz wondered idly as she soaped herself down. Toned and tanned, his abs and pecs were made out of steel; his muscles bulged like a proper man. When had she ever seen one of those before? Whatever prejudices Cassandra Bailey Brown had brought with her to Hawkshead, Caz Ryan had just ditched them. No one matched up to Galem, whatever his profession—no one even came close.

'Are you finished in there, or am I coming in?'

She laughed and ignored him; Galem would just have to wait. Her thoughts were abruptly truncated when the door lock flipped open and Galem stepped inside.

'How did you do that?' She caught her breath.

'I warned you about the water.' Parting the shower doors, he didn't hesitate. The way she'd brushed against him earlier had told him all he needed to know.

Her arms flew across her chest to cover it, and she was having difficulty balancing with her legs crossed.

'Something wrong, Caz?'

She lost, caught up by the very sight of him. He

looked better than she'd imagine. Quickly she tried to compose herself. 'Turn your back this instant.'

The last thing she had expected was for Galem's arm to sweep round her waist, or for his other hand to cup her head and drag her close. She should put up some resistance. She really should. She did. She placed both her hands flat against his powerful chest and gave him the feeblest push in her repertoire. It didn't work. By which time her fingers had closed on the crisp black hair on his chest and, instead of pushing him away, she was pulling him towards her... *And kissing him.*

They were bathed in steam as Galem's tongue lightly brushed her lips. It was better than the first time...this was the first time, or it felt like it. She felt as if she were melting from the inside out, every part of her on fire. She closed her eyes as Galem's strong white teeth closed lightly on her swollen bottom lip. His confidence, his strength, his power, she felt that he was placing all of it at her disposal.

He teased her as he always did, but not for so long. His breathing was just as hectic as hers, his need just as pressing. The sensation when his firm, warm hand started stroking the curve of her naked bottom was indescribable. He used long, even strokes that made her arch her back for him, asking for more. She was searching for more intimate touches, and tried desperately to press against him, but every time she got close Galem pulled away again. She rubbed her breasts against him, loving how tender her nipples had become. She loved to feel his rough chest hair scratching them. 'I want you,' she sighed, and reaching up, she wove her fingers through his thick, wet black hair. 'Kiss me, Galem,' she begged him. 'Kiss me properly.'

His answer was to hold her in front of him and as he stared down she said again, 'Kiss me…'

His wet mouth closed on her lips, sucking the last rational thought from her head. His face beard was rough against her face as she strained against him, and now she wanted to feel it over every part of her. She would never get enough of kissing him, tasting him, feeling him.

Pulling back when she could least bear it, he ran one firm thumb pad across the tender reddened skin beneath her mouth. 'Did I hurt you?'

She denied it fiercely, and brought him down to her again.

'I'll have to soothe it,' Galem breathed against her mouth.

'Only when you've kissed me all over,' Caz insisted, pressing against him.

'First I'm going soap you down,' he said, reaching for the sponge. 'Where would you like me to begin?'

'Anywhere you like… Just don't keep me waiting too long.'

Galem's smile was long and lazy as he charged the sponge. 'Vanilla and rosemary…'

He held it up for her to approve. She rested against him as he began.

'I think you like that,' he murmured.

She answered by parting her legs a little more, and then gasped for air as he made lazy circles round her breasts, teasing her nipples with the edge of the sponge until she was purring her satisfaction like a pampered pussy-cat.

'And how about this?' he said softly, running the sponge down the length of her back. She could only moan her pleasure when he reached her buttocks. Arching her back to its fullest extent, she felt the sponge slip down to where she so badly needed Galem to touch her. As she moved against him she could feel his erection pressing into her belly. He was enormous and her instinctive response was to draw back.

'Do I frighten you?'

'A little,' she admitted, burying her face in his chest.

Tipping her chin up, he cupped her face and kissed her again, very gently to reassure her, and then he deepened the kiss slowly until her fears had been left far behind. But he hadn't finished washing her and he started with her feet, moving on to her ankles, her calves, and then her thighs.

'More?' he murmured, as if asking her permission to continue.

'Just don't stop…'

He brushed her with the sponge intimately in a way that made her gasp. No one but Galem had ever touched her there before, but even as she was banking the sensation in her mind he pulled away and the spell was broken.

Rinsing out the sponge, he squeezed it dry, and, putting it back in the wire basket, he switched off the shower and reached outside for some towels. Dipping his head, he planted a tender kiss on the side of her neck. 'We need to get out of here before the water runs cold.'

That was no explanation. She watched him snatch up a robe and belt, and stood unresisting as he enveloped her in towels and lifted her into his arms. But as he carried her into the bedroom and lay her down gently on the bed her heart lifted and began beating so fast she could hardly think, hardly breathe. But instead of joining her he pulled up the blanket to cover her.

'Rest now…' His hand pressed her lightly as he turned to go.

'Galem, what did I do wrong?'

He hesitated a moment when she called him back, then, returning to the side of the bed, he sat down and took her hand, enclosing it in his. 'You're a virgin, Caz,' he said softly, shaking his head, angry with himself that he'd let things go this far.

To some men that might have represented an opportunity, Caz realised, but to Galem it was a barrier he wouldn't cross.

'Do you want to tell me about it?' he said, lifting his gaze from her hand to her face.

'Nothing to tell…' Her eyes widened. She was deeply embarrassed.

He had to keep reminding himself that her private life was no concern of his. But still he sensed that more than hard work and single-mindedness had kept her intact. It was as if she couldn't risk losing any part of her to another, as if she didn't quite believe in herself enough to do that. 'Caz, why are you here? And I don't just mean why are you here with me at the cottage right this minute. I mean what brought you to Hawkshead?' What drove you here? was what he meant, but he couldn't say that to her. She was too tender, too vulnerable.

'You know why I came,' she said, turning her face away. 'I inherited a house…'

She didn't want to talk to him about her past. She didn't want to talk about sex. She didn't want to open up to him, or anyone. She didn't know how, he realised. 'Why don't you sell Stone Break House and go back to the city—'

'Forget it,' she cut him off.

Were they both crazy fighting over a rambling ruin in the shadow of a quarry? Or were they fighting because it kept them together? There were no certainties any more.

The only thing he could be sure about was that she would continue to fight him, even if she couldn't explain why. Or maybe she could to herself. Maybe she had always wanted somewhere to call home, and Stone Break House just felt right to her.

'I'm keeping the house, and nothing you can say will change my mind.'

His internal temper flared at her defiance. He couldn't believe he had let things get this far, with Caz or with the house.

'My aunt must have had some reason for leaving the house to me,' she mused out loud, 'or why didn't she put it in the hands of her solicitor to sell with the rest of her effects?'

He softened as she looked at him, taking in the straight, no-nonsense nose, and the chin that looked as delicate as a china cup, until she jutted it out at him. She had the type of passion he always looked for in his executives, but how would she feel when she learned the truth about him? He had allowed things to go a lot further than he should have done.

'I don't know why Aunt Maud left Stone Break House to me,' she said, breaking into his thoughts, 'but whatever the reason I'm going to honour it.' He could see the determination in her eyes, but it masked a deeper sadness.

Honour? Galem ground his jaw as he took in what Caz had said. Where did honour lie in his father's mistress leaving her house to a niece she'd had no contact with? The solicitor had told him that much when he'd called to ask about the new owner.

Stone Break House was his. It had been his boyhood home, and it was wrapped up in the heritage he had come back to find, and finally understand. He had intended to make the new owner an offer they couldn't refuse. But now he couldn't just put the house out of his head—it meant too much to him. It was a symbol of his father's struggle to succeed, a struggle his late mother had shown no patience for.

Caz would have been different. The thought swept over him as he took in the firm set of her chin and the determination in her steady gaze. They'd have made a great team; it was just a pity they were pitted against each other.

She looked so small and pale in his big bed, so vulnerable. Her humiliation hovered over them like a dark cloud and for that he blamed himself. Self-control was his watchword, or had been until Caz had arrived in Hawkshead. Misleading her was a first for him; plus he'd hugely underestimated her determination. And he had almost given in to the temptation to sleep with her. He had no excuses for himself. He had picked up her sexual curiosity and naivety where men were concerned. He had picked up all the clues, but had simply chosen to ignore them.

CHAPTER TWELVE

DRAWING the blanket close, Caz looked up at Galem. 'I'm sorry, Galem.'

'What for?'

'I didn't mean to—' She could feel the sting of tears; it had all become too much.

'Didn't mean to what?' He took the blanket out of her fingers and pulled it up for her, as if she were a child who didn't know what was best for her.

'I didn't mean to make such a mess of things.'

'You didn't,' he told her frankly. He was the one to blame for that.

'Just tell me one thing, Galem.'

As she leaned forward he had to fight the temptation to take her in his arms. 'Tell you what?'

'We're still on for Stone Break House, aren't we?'

He bridled, then reminded himself that he wasn't the only one with feelings, but when she shot a bolt she hit the target every time. 'If I say I'll do something,' he told her firmly, 'I will. But I can't sleep with you, Caz, just so you can return to the office on Monday morning with a post-coital glow on your cheeks. And I won't sleep with you because you think your virginity is an embarrassment.'

'It isn't like that.' Her cheeks turned scarlet.

'I hope not.' He waited a few moments for her to compose herself. 'So why?'

'Why what?'

'How did you get to be this way, Caz—so defensive, so driven? Tell me about yourself. Did something bad happen?'

'No. Nothing like that.' Her eyes were wary as she made a gesture with her hand to dismiss his concern for her. Her body language told him more. It was a small movement, almost indiscernible, but she moved back as she protested, as if he'd hit a nerve. 'Tell me.'

'There's nothing to tell.'

'Okay.' He eased off. He'd go about it another way. 'I just thought we should get to know each other a little better if we're going to be working together, that's all. How about you give me three things that matter to you, three things you care about.'

Caz froze and then tried to moisten her lips with a tongue that had turned as dry as dust. Galem was employing the same interview technique Cassandra used. It was one that helped people to focus their thoughts and open up. Once they were relaxed the truth poured out. Or, as Cassandra would have put it, you lulled the candidate into a false sense of security with your apparent vagueness, and then went straight for the jugular. She didn't like being in the firing line—how could she when her life was built on a lie? At the office Cassandra talked warmly about her supportive family, and of course she had attended an exclusive girls' school. Then there was the family membership at the tennis club and the golf club, the annual ski trip, and the villa in Portugal. Caz Ryan was a fast learner and she had soon found out what it took to fit in with the high-flying set at the top of the tree. Fortunately, no one had ever called her bluff. Why should they, when she spoke as they did, wore the appropriate uniform, and dropped the right names? They accepted her as one of them. Cassandra Bailey Brown was 'in'.

And it all counted for nothing, Caz reflected as Galem waited for her answer. The only thing she wanted now was to tell the truth to this man. But if she did he wouldn't understand. She knew for a fact that Galem would hate pretension, and would think her a fool for ever courting it.

'Can't you think of three things?' he pressed.

'Of course I can.' She ticked them off on her fingers, staring him straight in the eyes, knowing he would root out any deception right away. 'Family…' The family she longed for. 'Loyalty…' To that family. 'And…' She was about to say 'love', and then quickly changed it to 'Stone Break House', adding, 'The moment I saw the house it was love at first sight.'

The look in Galem's eyes had made her say it. Whatever he said she knew he wanted Stone Break House for himself. And why was she the only one under the spotlight here? 'And now it's your turn to come up with three things.'

Briefly she thought he might refuse, but then the humour came back into his eyes. 'Okay,' he said, falling in with her. 'I care about my work, the people I work with, and everything else that falls within my sphere of influence.'

Galem's sphere of influence? Caz felt vaguely disappointed. She had expected more passion from him; more insights into who he was. 'Game over?' she said, wanting to move things on, to get out of his bed and put some clothes on while she still had a shred of pride intact.

'Game over,' he agreed, refusing to break eye contact so it was far from over.

She took the cue for Stone Break House and ran with it. 'If we could have a look round the house tomorrow, say around lunchtime, we could draw up a schedule of work so when I go back to Leeds I can put a proposal in front of my bank manager.'

'Okay by me.'

He was still staring at her, and the air was still charged. She still craved his warmth. Too bad. She went to get out of bed. They both moved at the same time and the space around them shrank to nothing. Their faces were millimetres apart, their lips almost touching.

'Caz, no…'

Galem drew his head back and lifted his hands away from her, holding them out as if signalling his promise not to touch her. She didn't move. 'Why not?' The words were barely spoken but they hovered in the air between them like an unspoken pledge.

He held her eye contact, and it felt to Caz as if he could see right into her soul. She had lied to him about who she was but she couldn't lie about how she felt. Drawing her hand up to his face, she made the first move. Grazing her fingers down his roughened jaw, she was nervous, but she didn't want this to end. As if he sensed this, Galem leant forward and brushed the hair from her brow, and then he drew her slowly and very tenderly into his arms. His kisses made her relax. He feathered them over her eyelids and her cheeks, and on down her neck, then, pulling her up the bed, he cupped her face in his hands and brushed her lips with his mouth. 'Are you sure?' he whispered, sending a trail of fire down her arms with his fingertips.

Lacing their fingers together, he kissed her again. His restraint was arousing her beyond anything she had ever known. She nodded and started to say something, but Galem put a finger over her lips, and then he replaced that finger with his mouth, kissing the fear out of her.

Tenderness was something she had never experienced and had never anticipated. It brought tears to her eyes, and made a nonsense of all the brash talk at the office about Saturday night clinches and fast, fierce couplings. This was different, very different, this was something that grabbed at her heart and squeezed it tight.

'Touch me…' She strained against him, lacing her fingers through his hair, flying high on the point of giving away something so precious and integral, but feeling it was so right. It was a huge step to take, but at that moment it felt like the easiest decision she'd ever made. It was a step she knew now that Cassandra could never take, because Cassandra had nothing to give. And Caz wanted to give everything she had, everything she was, to Galem. He made her feel so safe, cherished, precious, all she wanted was to be enveloped in his warmth, his power, his gentle strength.

'Listen to your body,' he murmured as she cried out with pleasure. 'There's no rush…'

Easy for him to say, but her body was clamouring with sensation and she wanted more, but Galem was pacing her and so she had to be content with his chaste kisses until she grew quiet again.

'Good girl,' he murmured, stroking her.

How much longer could she bear the frustration? She gave a gasp of relief when his hands started a more interesting track over her belly, and eased her thighs apart to draw his attention. 'Stop teasing me…'

'I want this to be special for you, and if you don't lie still—'

'You'll what?' she challenged softly.

Seizing her wrists for answer, he fastened them in his fist above her head, resting them on the soft bank of pillows. 'You asked for this…'

'You wouldn't dare tease me…'

Drawing one of her nipples into his mouth, he proved he would. He suckled hard, showing her no mercy, and then made sure the other one received the same attention.

'I love your breasts,' he said, pulling back to admire them. 'They're magnificent.'

She didn't want him staring, she wanted him doing, and bucked towards him to give him a hint.

His eyes were laughing as he stared down at her. 'So magnificent I think just looking at them might be enough for me.'

'No,' she warned succinctly.

With a soft laugh Galem returned to his duties, and by the time he'd finished with her both her nipples were hard and pink. Gleaming wet, they stood extended and provocative. 'I want you,' she said, reaching for him. 'Don't make me wait.'

'In the workplace you may be used to people obeying you, but in my bed you do as you're told.'

He made a pass across her nipples with the rough stubble on his chin, reducing her in that one move to a whimpering, writhing ferment of sensation.

'Tell me what you want,' he insisted. 'You have to tell me, Caz.'

'You know what I want…'

'Tell me…'

His voice had a harder edge that turned her on.

'I want you, Galem. I want you now…'

'And what do you want with me?' His lips tugged up.

'You know what I want…'

'Do I?'

'Please stop teasing me.'

'And do what?'

'Make love to me…'

'Like this?' he suggested, slipping lower in the bed.

'Oh, yes…yes.' She cried out with pleasure and relief as his tongue found her. 'Please don't stop…' She couldn't bear it; she wasn't sure it was possible to withstand so much pleasure, but she was prepared to try.

Lacing her fingers through Galem's thick black hair, she kept him tightly in place. His tongue was warm and firm and rough, everything she wanted, and this time he didn't deny her anything.

She cried out, convulsing on the bed in the throes of pleasure so intense, so enduring, she wondered if she would survive. He let her down gently and then held her for a while until she was still.

'Good…'

'Mmm,' she managed, utterly contented and ready to fall asleep in his arms. But then he started kissing her again in a way that very soon made her strain against him.

She felt bereft when he sat up, and then went very still, hearing a foil rip. He came back to her immediately, stroking her face. 'Do you trust me?'

She gazed steadily into his eyes. 'You know I do.'

He kissed her again, tenderly, gently, and while he was kissing her his hand found her. She went to say something and couldn't. Her need was so great, the hunger had returned, and Galem was stroking her delicately and deliberately, drawing more exquisite sensation out of her than she had known was possible. The pleasure spread out in rippling waves until she relaxed completely into it, wondering at the destination, and only fearing that if it was in any way better than this she might pass out before she got there.

When Galem moved on top of her he was kissing her at the same time, kissing her, stroking her, soothing. Looking deep into her eyes, he cupped her buttocks and she felt a wonderful pressure that coaxed every part of her into readiness to receive him.

She drew her legs back, wanting nothing to stand in their way, and her breathing quickened in preparation for what was to come.

Testing her readiness, he pulled back at first, making her cry out with disappointment, but then he set up a gentle rocking motion stroking her, and it allowed her to take as much or as little of him as she wanted to. When he was sure she was ready he moved deeper still, and so he took her without pain.

Caz's lips parted in surprise as Galem stretched her for the first time. The sensation was incredible. He was so careful, so gentle and considerate. He kissed her over and over, his words caressed her, and her body responded to him as he set up a steady rhythm. There was more tenderness in his eyes than she had ever seen before, and it was that look that made her lose control. Calling out his name repeatedly, she shuddered and bucked in the intense throes of pleasure, only to collapse exhausted and replete in his arms.

They slept for a while wound around each other, and she woke to find Galem caressing her again. 'I can't,' she insisted sleepily, rolling onto her stomach.

'Is that a fact?'

She barely had strength to move her head on the pillow, but she turned it to the side and opened her eyes to stare at him. 'All right, maybe I can,' she mumbled, closing her eyes again, feigning sleep. But Galem had started stroking her bottom again, and somehow her legs parted without her having anything to do with it. 'How did you do that?' she asked him groggily, barely opening her eyes or her mouth. 'And don't you dare say years of training…'

'Let's just call it a natural talent, shall we?' Galem suggested, drawing her beneath him.

He sank inside her, pressing deep. 'Is that too much for you?'

He'd asked because she was clinging to him, gasping for breath. 'I just need a second. I can't think, can't breathe…'

'Breathe, don't think,' he advised, starting to move again.

She groaned with pleasure as Galem filled her, massaging her inside and out with each thrust. But then he did something that made her cry out in complaint. 'You love teasing me, don't you?' she accused him as he withdrew completely and made her wait before re-entering her again so very slowly.

'I love to bring you pleasure; I love to watch that pleasure unfold on your face.'

Pressing her knees back, Galem knelt between her legs, proving just how much pleasure she could take. Her cries halted him.

'Have I hurt you?'

'Don't stop!' she warned him furiously, in a real panic that he might. She was developing quite an appetite.

But as he kissed her this time Caz felt that everything had changed. And not just her virginal state. She knew Galem was wrong for her, totally wrong for her, they were wrong for each other, but she was in very real danger of falling in love with him.

'Caz…'

He was moving steadily now, firmly, drawing her attention to his eyes. Drawing her once again to the height of passion.

'How do you do that?' she asked him later when they were quiet.

'How do I do what?' Galem murmured lazily.

'All you have to do is prompt me, and I—'

'Obey?' he suggested, receiving a nudge of disapproval for his trouble.

'You know what I mean,' Caz insisted, finding it
an effort to move her mouth and keep her eyes open
at the same time.

'Don't you like my suggestions?'

'Love them…' She smiled into his eyes.

'That's what I thought. So here's another one…'

She was instantly awake as Galem eased onto
his back. She trusted him absolutely, but she was still
in beginner's class. 'Can I…can I do this?'

'Do you want to try?'

She straddled him. 'So are you just going to lie
there?' She had forgotten how big he was, and,
having sampled the tip, she drew back.

Taking her in his arms, Galem swung her beneath
him. 'Shall I show you again?'

'I think you better had. I'm a slow learner…'

'Don't worry, you've got all night to get it right.'

'I was hoping you might say that.'

'Hold me, Caz…'

She needed both her hands to encompass his
girth, but it was worth it to explore the silky hardness
ridged with veins. From base to tip it was quite a
journey. 'May I?' she asked politely.

'Be my guest…' Galem's lips pressed down in
a contented smile as she began. Drawing him in,
she closed her muscles around him. 'You're my
prisoner now.'

'I yield,' he assured her. 'Is that good?'

'Perfect.'

'A little deeper, perhaps?'

'How deep?'

'Are you ready to find out?'

'I wouldn't miss it for the world.' Caz felt joy soar inside her.

'I might lose control,' he warned.

'You're not allowed until I say you can.'

'And when will that be?'

'Never.'

'How much do you want of me, Caz?'

'All of you... I want it all.'

Oh, God, she meant it. She meant it. She really meant it. She hoped Galem couldn't read her mind. She had never exposed her vulnerable inner self to another human being before in her life, and yet just now in the throes of making love with Galem she had made the most honest declaration of her life.

CHAPTER THIRTEEN

THEY woke to sunshine streaming into the bedroom early on Sunday morning.

'I should be getting back,' Caz said reluctantly.

'Who says so?'

Galem was right. There was no rigid timetable in Hawkshead for her to follow.

'The freedom here is what I appreciate most,' he said, as if he'd picked up on her thoughts. Sitting up in bed, he was gazing out across the moors.

Was that why he was content to stay here? Caz wondered, dropping kisses on his shoulder.

'We have to go to the house yet,' he reminded her, easing her down on the bed. 'So you might as well plan on staying in Hawkshead for a bit longer.'

How was she supposed to think about leaving when Galem was kissing her neck? 'I couldn't possibly impose on you,' she teased him.

'But I want you to.' His mouth tugged up into the

familiar wicked smile. 'You may have to stay the night too…'

'Really?' Sucking in a deep breath, she tried to keep her thoughts confined to the conversation, but that was impossible now Galem was moving down the bed. She capitulated gracefully. 'Oh, all right, then,' she agreed.

'First one into the shower,' Caz suggested round about noon.

But Galem had played the game before with her, and as she launched herself off the bed he came after her.

'Room for two?' he said, holding the shower door as she tried to close it in his face.

That wasn't a question, Caz realised as Galem joined her. She backed into a corner, inviting him to come closer.

'You don't mind sharing the shower, do you?' he said, turning it on.

Caz screamed and launched herself at him as freezing cold water cascaded down on them.

'I'd better warm you up,' Galem offered.

'You better had,' Caz threatened, scrambling up him.

He took her there in the shower, holding her off the ground, two strong hands clamped to her buttocks while she braced her feet against the wall. Freezing outside and hot inside was quite a combination. It was incredible. He was incredible, and addictive, Caz mused when Galem let her down gently and started kissing her.

'Why, Cassandra,' Galem drawled, holding Caz in front of him while a substantial natural divide was still holding them apart, 'I do believe you're blushing.'

For once he was wrong; Cassandra would have fainted. 'I'm not blushing. The shower's turned hot.'

'So, you'll stay?' he guessed.

Was there any doubt? Raising her arms to slick her hair back in a gesture Caz realised was deliberately provocative, she licked her lips to ramp up the pressure. 'If you can take the pace?'

'I'll hold up.'

She was sure of it.

Galem pushed the doors open. 'Now, get out of here, or we'll never go see that house.'

After breakfast Caz suggested a picnic to tie in with their visit to the house.'

'A walk, at least,' Galem agreed, brushing her swollen bottom lip with his thumb pad.

They could hardly keep their hands off each other and a rosy glow had descended on them by the time they left the cottage arm in arm.

'Why are you stopping?' He turned to stare at her when they were halfway up a hill overlooking the quarry.

'I'm admiring the view.'

'Again?'

'Is there a limit?' She couldn't disguise her gulping breaths any longer. She needed a break.

'I thought you were fit.' Galem's laugh was deep and sexy, and it resonated through her.

'For pavements.' She smiled ruefully. These hills were steeper than the treadmill at the city gym. But as Galem drew her close Caz knew she wouldn't have missed this for the world.

'Can you see the house?' he said, turning her. 'It's why I brought you here.'

Caz found herself watching Galem's face instead of looking down on Stone Break House. She loved him; it was that simple and that complicated. There was an edge of darkness hovering at the edges of her happiness because when it came to Stone Break House Galem's sense of ownership equalled her own.

She just had to put it out of her mind and get on with things, Caz told herself, looking for a place to sit as she waited for Galem.

'Not there!'

His shout was too late to prevent her sitting in a mud bath that might have been tailor-made for her bottom.

Grabbing her underneath the arms, Galem went to yank her up. 'Can't leave you alone for a second, can I, Cassandra?'

She stared into his eyes, thinking. Cassandra had been accident-proof; she'd had to be. But Caz…she was different.

'Well?' Galem said. 'Do you want to get up or not?'

His thick black hair was ruffled by the wind and his profile was a sharply carved silhouette against a white sky. There was such strength in his jaw, such kindness and humour in his eyes, and for once she didn't want to do what was right or sensible. 'Do you fancy getting really muddy?'

His eyes turned slumberous in an expression she recognised, but then he threw back his head and laughed, understanding.

The ground was soft and warm and as they wrestled Caz knew it was the most fun she'd ever had. 'Now I know why mud treatments are so popular,' she said, gasping for breath when Galem allowed her to hold him down. 'Do you think our clothes will ever recover?'

'I'm guessing you hope not,' he said, drawing her to him for a kiss.

And then he held her and she lay safe in his arms swimming in a warm, safe tide of love. Being hugged by Galem, being kissed by him, seeing the affection in his eyes when he looked at her, meant more to Caz than anything. It meant more to her than Stone Break House, more than losing her virginity even. Affection; respect; trust. However short a time they'd known each other it was all there, and she valued it above everything.

'Come on,' he said, getting up and drawing her to her feet.

'I've never had a muddy kiss before,' Caz said as Galem cupped her face in his big, muddy hands.

'Then let me be the first,' he whispered against her lips.

'This is the best day of my life,' Caz said when Galem released her at last.

'All that could change in a moment,' he warned, turning her to point out the black cloud heading their way.

'But the forecast promised—' Caz stopped. Since when had she believed in weather predictions?

'If we hurry we might get back before the downpour.'

'And if we don't?'

'We'll get wet.' The crease was back in Galem's cheek again.

They set off down the hill at a brisk pace, but there were a lot of damp leaves underfoot, and damp leaves under Caz's trainers were a recipe for disaster.

'You really can't be trusted for a moment, can you?' Galem said, scooping her off the ground a second time.

Caz brushed herself down, glad of the opportunity to hide her face. She didn't want Galem thinking she was the type of girl who took a tumble and burst into tears, though right now that was exactly the type of girl she was. What had happened to Cassandra when she needed her? Caz seemed to be losing her poise and pride by the minute.

'Take it slowly,' Galem advised, keeping a protective arm around her shoulders. 'Get your wind back.'

'But the rain—' Breaking free, she set off again.

'Caz, watch out! Don't go that way!'

'Why not?' The way she had chosen was prettier than the track Galem was taking. There were wild-flowers and…thistles!

'Or that way!'

Nettles!

'Ouch!' Galem said it for her. 'Now will you stay with me?'

For ever, Caz thought as she gazed up into his face, but, of course, she didn't say that.

'We have a stream to cross now,' Galem informed her when they reached the bottom of the hill, 'and I don't want you trying any heroics. You're to take my hand so I can get you safely to the other side.'

The stones were slippery, but Galem's arm was like a steel rod, his hand like a grappling iron welded to a winch of limitless strength. She wasn't sur-prised he brought her safely over to the other side. She only wished the stream had been wider; the Atlantic Ocean, perhaps.

The sight of Stone Break House from the top of the hill had only increased his passion for it; seeing it with Caz had only aggravated his dilemma. She was never going to sell, and he was never going to give up his rights to it either. It was an impossible situa-tion made worse by her stubbornness. Made worse by the way she made him feel, Galem admitted to himself. Who in their right mind would want to make their home in an old ruin that was overshadowed by the gaping wound of a former quarry? Only the man who had lived there as a boy, perhaps…

Until Caz had come along, that was. She felt so good in his arms. Better than that, she felt right there. But she knew that if he told her how he felt she would think it a ploy to claim Stone Break House through the back door. Things got complicated when your father's mistress turned out to have a niece as beautiful and complicated as Cassandra Bailey Brown, a woman whom he would always think of as Caz…

'Breather?' she begged him.

'When it rains here it really rains,' he warned her.

'Oh, not like anywhere else, then,' she said, laughing into his eyes.

She tempted him, and he dropped a kiss on her lips, loving the easy familiarity that had sprung up between them. He'd never felt like this before. Sex, lust, accommodations between a man and a woman, those he understood, but this…this was something very different.

He waited until she recovered, feeling like a jerk. He was in a mess. He was pushing her too hard. What had started out as an undercover interview once he'd realised who she was on Friday night had become something more, something that made him push her to see what she was really made of. She was such an enigma, but he preferred what he had now to what had landed in his ditch on Friday night.

'Is it much further, Galem?'

Her jaw was jutting out in a way that made him smile. 'Just one tiny field,' he said, using a little poetic licence. 'Get your breath back first, and then we'll set off again.'

He helped her over a stile when they reached the field. Her clothes were sodden from the mud, but he could feel her warmth beneath them. It reminded him how good she felt when she was naked. He was just making some discreet adjustments when she froze.

'Galem, what are those?'

They had only gone a few yards into the field. He followed her gaze to see a herd of bullocks lifting their heads from the grass to take an interest in them. 'Don't worry,' he said with all the confidence of a man who used to sneak a ride as a boy. 'They won't hurt you.'

'Are you mad?' she said, looking at him horror struck.

Before he had chance to say another word she took off, legs working like pistons as she ran in the opposite direction to the way they should be going.

'Cows can kill…'

Cupping his hands around his mouth, he yelled back at her, 'Only if you're careless. And those aren't cows, they're—'

'Chasing me.'

'No, they're not,' he said, loping after her. He threw a glance over his shoulder to be sure, only to see a small stampede forming up. 'Okay, they are! Make for the trees!'

But she couldn't run fast enough. He guessed her legs had turned to rubber and he could hear the drum of hooves coming up behind them fast. Sweeping her up beneath one arm, he carried her like a rugby ball to touchdown.

'Idiot!' she screamed when he landed on top of her.

He had to admit it wasn't quite the show of gratitude he had anticipated.

'How could you bring me to a field that had rampaging bulls in it?'

'Bullocks—'

'Dangerous animals!'

Capturing her flailing arms, he forced them into a puddle above her head. 'Cassandra, calm down…'

'Get off me, you great oaf!' she said, wriggling furiously.

She had never been rugby-tackled before; never been thrown to the ground by a grown man, never wrestled twice in one day in soft warm mud before. And wrestling with Galem meant extremely impressionable parts of her were rubbing into him again and again. 'Galem, I'm warning you—' *If you stop holding me down and pressing yourself against me, I'll kill you!*

They stopped fighting and she grew quiet. They

were looking into each other's eyes, really looking. Galem's green eyes were deep and mesmerising, and that mouth… They'd have gorgeous children. Swallowing hard, Caz forced the thought from her mind, but the shared dangerous incident had brought them even closer. 'The last thing I want to do is mud wrestle with you again,' she assured him in a way that brought the familiar crease to his cheek.

'Now, why don't I believe you?'

She melted into his arms when Galem bent his head and kissed her. 'You feel so good,' she murmured, sighing as she rubbed herself against him. 'I want to feel you all over me.'

'I love it when we think the same,' Galem murmured against her mouth.

He was making her ready as he spoke, undoing the fastening on her polyester trousers, and freeing the zip. She opened the buttons on his shirt and pulled up her top so she could feel him hard and warm against her.

Even on a bed of mud their love-making was sensual and tender. They knew each other's bodies, knew each other now. This was falling in love, Caz thought as Galem sank deep inside her, holding her gaze. This was what it felt like to be loved, and to love, heart soaring, body thrilling, mind flying. Oblivious to the sullen sky, she dug her fingertips into the bulging muscles beneath Galem's shirt, loving him for ever with all her heart.

As she relaxed back in his arms, panting and

glowing, he couldn't believe they'd known each other such a short time. She was different from every woman he had ever met; she fulfilled all his fantasies, ticked each box on his wish list. She was gutsy, sexy and stubborn, and stirred his competitive juices like no one he'd ever met. That wasn't just a change—for him it was unique. He was a little bit in love with her, and maybe a lot more than that. And that wasn't just his libido talking. When she'd first arrived his mind had been full of Stone Break House and he had bitterly resented her for owning it, but now he could have it all.

'Is it really only Sunday afternoon?' he murmured against her sweet flushed face. 'So we've known each other—'

She was brushing damp strands of hair out of her eyes, and, catching hold of her wrist, he brought her palm to his lips and planted a kiss on it. 'I don't care how long. It's long enough for me.'

Caz tensed, wondering what Galem meant by that. Even now insecurity was waiting in the wings ready to raise its ugly head. 'Long enough for what?' She held her breath, dreading his answer. She had travelled a long way since arriving in Hawkshead and she was miles past worrying about being in too deep.

'Long enough to know I don't want to let you go,' he said, drawing her close. 'Long enough to know I want to know you a whole lot better than I do…'

When they were dressed again he brought her

onto his knees, holding her on his lap in his big strong arms like a baby beneath the spreading branches of an ancient oak. 'It doesn't get any better than this, does it?' she said, turning her face up to him.

Galem's answer was to kiss her, and they kissed like lovers who had known each other a lot longer than a few hours. There was a new certainty between them and a sense of trust, a growing knowledge that every moment they spent together brought them closer.

A new horizon full of possibilities had opened up for her, and Caz found it hard to believe she had ever thought them mismatched. Galem was the builder and she was the dreamer; he was the man who would build her dreams. And her dreams encompassed a lot more now than an old house. She was about to tell him how much she loved him when Galem stared at her and grinned. 'Ready, Cassandra? Shall we start back?'

Calling her Cassandra brought her back to earth with a bump. This was all a sham. Galem had made love to her and spent time with her, because he wanted Stone Break House. He wanted Cassandra. He wanted a girl who didn't exist. How could she have forgotten that?

Because she wanted to, Caz realised. She wanted all the things she'd never had. In fairness to him Galem had never mentioned love once. Perhaps she expected too much of him, Caz thought as they started back, expected too much of life…

She tried not to think too hard about it as she matched her stride to his, but everything inside her had grown cold and tight. When she was in his arms Galem made her feel as if she were the only woman in the world, but Galem lived a simple life, and sex for him was just part of the natural rhythm of that life. She mustn't read too much into what had happened between them that weekend. It might have been earth-shattering for her, but for him it was probably different.

'Why don't we go and look at Stone Break House now, if you have to get back to Leeds?' he said.

The way he spoke underlined her fears. The weekend was drawing to a close and with it his commitment to her. He was already prepared in his mind for her leaving, while she couldn't bear to think about it. 'You're right,' she said, hiding behind Cassandra's no-nonsense tone. But this time the switch grated on her. She didn't want to go back to being the person she had been on Friday night at the start of this journey.

When they reached the gates of the house Galem touched her shoulder as if he sensed her anxiety without understanding the cause of it. It was the type of touch a man might give to a colleague to reassure her—brief and impersonal. Before she could stop herself she caught hold of his hand and kissed the fingertips that had brought her so much pleasure. She loved him however he felt about her, and there were still a few hours remaining. Whatever the future held she would put it out of her mind for now.

CHAPTER FOURTEEN

THE list of 'things to do' at Stone Break House was growing longer by the minute, though Galem insisted that none of the tasks was impossible. She needed his enthusiasm and energy to buoy her up, Caz realised, especially on those occasions in the future when her money ran low, or when, temporarily, she lost faith.

'The way forward is to restore rather than rip out and start again,' he commented, leading her round the back of the house. 'That way we can preserve the unique character of the building.'

The unique character of the building. Even the way he talked about the house showed his love for it. She had to wonder at the depth of Galem's attachment to a pile of old stones and rotting timbers. She had to wonder at the depth of her love for him too. Could this really have happened in a weekend? It had, she realised, taking his hand.

Galem laced their fingers together in an intimate

gesture that made her long to ask him if he felt the same way she did. It cut her up inside to think there was always part of her she would have to keep hidden from him.

'I wouldn't be surprised if we could reclaim the tennis court,' he said, reclaiming her attention.

'The tennis court?' Her brow wrinkled. He was directing her attention to what looked to her like a wilderness of broken fences and weeds. She hadn't allowed for anything like a tennis court in her budget. 'That will have to wait...'

'Perhaps we can sort something out,' he said.

What did he mean by that? She flashed a glance at him. Then as the breeze lifted her hair from her face she turned to gaze out at the miles of rolling fields, a patchwork of green and gold.

'Happy?' Galem said, drawing her close.

Happier than you know, Caz thought, snuggling into him. Nothing could spoil this moment, she wouldn't let it. She set her mind free to picture the ponies and sheep that would graze in the fields. 'We even have enough land to run a sanctuary,' she said, speaking her thoughts out loud.

'A sanctuary? What kind of sanctuary?'

'For animals,' she said, turning to him, warming to her theme.

'Go on,' Galem prompted.

Maybe he would think it sounded silly. She firmed her jaw. 'A home for racing greyhounds when they retire... Or donkeys. I love donkeys.'

Galem's expression changed and softened as he stared at the waiting land. 'My father started his business on the proceeds of the winnings from Stone Break Sid's ancestor, so yes…' His voice died away.

'The building business?' she probed, seizing the single strand from his life and clinging to it.

'That's right.'

'So you think my idea might work?'

'It has possibilities.'

'I wish I didn't have to go back to Leeds…'

'And work?'

She sounded like a spoiled child, Caz realised, but she was itching to make a start here.

'You'll make new friends in the north.'

She only wanted him. Her eyes filled. She turned her face away so he couldn't see. All she wanted was to be the real Caz Ryan with Galem. And self-pity was no use to anyone. 'I already have made friends,' she said to jolt herself out of it.

It made her smile to think about her new colleagues at the Leeds office. Fun and uninhibited, none of the girls cared what accent you had. They liked labels as much as the next, but weren't afraid to augment their shopping with supermarket bargains to get the latest look. They were real people and she had envied them from the moment she'd walked into the office.

'Caz?' Galem prompted her gently.

She looked up at him, shrewd green eyes that saw so much, and wanted to tell him everything, but if she did that she had to admit to being a fake. It was a vicious circle from which there was no escape. And Galem was as elusive as she was. How much had she learned about him since they'd met?

They both turned and frowned at the unwelcome intrusion of a car horn.

'Oh, no,' Caz sighed.

'Are you expecting visitors?' Galem asked her as a flashy red sports car zoomed up to them.

'Surprise!' a woman screeched as it skidded to a halt throwing a spray of gravel in the air. Leaning out of the passenger window, she waved a bottle of champagne in Caz's face.

'Cordelia Wentworth-Smythe,' she shrilled, holding out one beautifully manicured hand to Galem.

There was a moment when Caz thought Galem was going to salute her, but somehow he held back. They must look a sight, she realised, after rolling in the mud, whereas Cordelia and Hugo, both colleagues from the London office, were as immaculately dressed as ever. They climbed out of the car, looked around and then at each other.

'Fresh supplies!' Cordelia announced, putting on a brave face. Turning her back on Galem, she handed the bottle of champagne to Caz.

Cordelia had already dismissed Galem on the flimsy evidence of his rough appearance and muddy clothes. The spell they had woven between them during the weekend was shattered; the past had

caught up with them. As Cordelia swept a posses-
sive arm around her waist and led her away Caz
wondered if she would survive this visit, or if
Cassandra would seize this opportunity to take her
over completely.

'You didn't think we'd forget you, did you,
darling?' Cordelia flashed a glance at Galem over
her shoulder. 'Just tell me if we're in the way.'

Cordelia would have been too much at any time.

'You must have known we wouldn't abandon you
in the country?' she went on, this time staring pointedly at Galem.

Caz felt instantly protective towards him.

'Cassandra, your clothes—'

'They're practical.' The edge to her voice made
Cordelia's eyebrows shoot up.

'That's exactly what I mean.'

As Cordelia's eyes closed briefly in disapproval
Caz thought the expression in Galem's eyes spoke
volumes about his opinion of her London chums. And
it was as if she was seeing them clearly for the first
time. Hugo had just stepped out of the car and was re-
garding Galem as if he had only recently climbed out
of the swamp. In some ways he was right, Caz thought,
smothering her smile. But Hugo and Cordelia's pretensions grated on her, and she was mortified to think
that only a short while before she had felt the same.
But they were here, and she had to remember her
manners. 'Welcome, Hugo,' she said, fixing a smile
to her face. 'You've driven a long way to see me.'

'We were curious,' Hugo admitted frankly. The look he gave Stone Break House made Caz's hackles rise. She could feel Galem seething beside her too, and to avoid direct conflict between the two men she decided introductions were in order. 'Hugo, I'd like to introduce—'

'You can introduce us to the staff later,' Hugo cut across her.

His accent might have been cultivated in richly furnished drawing rooms rather than muddy fields, but as far as she was concerned Hugo's manners stank, but her scowl of disapproval seemed to bounce off him, making no effect whatsoever.

'I'll leave you with your friends…'

'No, Galem.'

He ignored her outstretched hand. She was proud of him. Galem had remained cool and dignified throughout. He had made a point of acknowledging Hugo and Cordelia, whether they cared to be acknowledged or not, and as he walked away she wanted to shout, 'Wait for me! These people aren't my friends. I don't know what I was thinking about.' But she had extended an open invitation to Hugo and Cordelia to visit her any time. She couldn't turn her back on them now.

Be honest for once, Caz thought as she watched Galem's retreating back. The truth was she didn't have the guts to stand up to Hugo and Cordelia and destroy her precious image.

Her image? Caz gazed down at her ruined

clothes, and then glanced at Hugo and Cordelia. Galem was long gone, his easy loping stride eating up the distance between her and his destination, which was almost certainly the cottage.

She had just made the most monumental mistake of her life, Caz realised. Galem was the one genuine thing in that life, the rock she could build on, and she had thrown all that away for the sake of her pride.

But not if she acted quickly enough. Caz firmed her jaw. She would just have to tell Hugo and Cordelia this was a bad time and she had to leave. The only thing that mattered now was straightening things out with Galem before she left for Leeds.

It wasn't hard to apologise and recommend a smart hotel in the centre of Leeds—in fact she couldn't believe what a relief it had been. Now she only had to find Galem, put her arms around him and assure him that nothing had changed.

So why did she still have the nagging feeling that the bottom had just dropped out of her world?

Caz walked all the way back to the cottage, and was devastated to find it empty. The silence was intense, just as she remembered it when she had first arrived. She had been so concerned with her own timetable, she hadn't given a thought to Galem's, she realised. In her mind he was a fixture, a paver who lived in a gorgeous little cottage. But what did she really know about him?

And she was supposed to be an expert when it came to reading people? Caz was angry with herself as she stuffed her scant possessions into the ruined bag. Cassandra, you're a washout, and you'd better pull yourself together before work tomorrow morning. Dashing the tears from her eyes, she took one last look around the room where her life had changed for good, then, swinging her bag off the floor, she went downstairs to call a taxi.

'Station, love?'

She was on the point of saying yes, but what came out of her mouth was, 'No... Could you take me to Stone Break House, please?' Maybe Galem was there; she didn't know where else to look.

'Stone Break House?' the taxi driver said in surprise. 'That old ruin?'

'It won't be for much longer,' Caz assured him, narrowing her gaze. 'And that's where I'd like you to take me now, please.'

When they arrived she paid off the taxi driver and, using her keys, walked inside. She called out for him, but she already knew he wasn't there; she would have felt his presence, had he been.

She made a tour of the house, being careful to avoid all the places Galem had warned her about. It wasn't so bad if she was careful. A fanciful side of her imagined she could hear laughter and voices; happy voices; a family... Leaning back against the door jamb, Caz pictured the large open-plan kitchen area as it would be when she had finished with it.

There would be an Aga at one end, and a wood-burning stove at the other with two sofas pulled up either side. In the winter she'd have rugs and candles and throws…

It would be lovely, Caz thought, biting her lips against the tears that threatened when she thought how much lovelier it could have been with Galem to share it with. Thinking about him now made her throat tighten and her heart ache. Another lesson learned; he hadn't even bothered to say goodbye.

And so she was alone again. But maybe that was enough. Staying here in the house where she felt she belonged was a consolation of sorts. Having accepted that, the rest was easy. She was going to stay the night, and not just Sunday night, but every weekend from now on. She didn't feel frightened by the old house any more. The wildlife was probably a lot more frightened of her than she was of it.

An old sofa faced the black iron grate, and that was where she would make her bed for the night. When she went back to Leeds she would arrange to have it recovered, and have another one made to match it. Galem was right about saving everything that could be saved. She wanted as much as he did to keep the spirit of the house intact.

CHAPTER FIFTEEN

'THERE was no more to your trip than a country hike, I bet,' her PA commented, on Monday morning when Caz walked into Brent Construction. 'Something's put that glow on your cheeks…' She smiled, sharing a knowing look with the other girls.

Like a perfectly schooled chorus line they all craned forward to hear what she had to say.

Caz managed a smile. 'If there was, I'm not telling.'

'You don't have to,' the chorus assured her.

Closing her office door with relief, Caz hit the intercom button. 'No calls, please, Julie…' She needed a minute before buckling on her business armour, a minute to mourn. The girls were right—she was glowing, but that glow was fading fast. She'd hardly slept for thinking about Galem, and what a fool she'd made of herself. She'd bought into the fable of love at first sight, which she now knew was a lie.

'When you're ready,' Caz said, hitting the intercom button again, 'a coffee would be great, Julie. And I'm taking calls now.'

'Don't forget your ten o'clock—'

'My ten o'clock?' Her mind turned blank for a moment, but then she remembered, wondering at the same time how she could possibly have forgotten. 'Young Mr Brent?'

'That's right,' Julie confirmed.

A visit from Mr Brent had been on the cards for some time. He'd been out of the country for years, growing the business into a world class concern, but now he was back. 'Better hold those calls a few more minutes, Julie.' She needed to be on top form for this meeting.

Ten minutes later Caz slammed her file shut. How was she supposed to concentrate? With an angry sound she thrust her chair back from the desk and started pacing. Galem's face, Galem's eyes, Galem's lips, Galem's body... Galem the bit of rough she had fallen madly in love with; Galem the bad boy who had turned his back on her without a second thought; Galem the unrepentant alpha, the lusted-after sex toy with his long, lean legs, powerful arms and incredible iron buttocks; Galem, the man composed entirely of muscle and appetite, with no finer feelings at all. How was she supposed to forget about someone like that and concentrate on work?

'Julie? Coffee; it's an emergency. And those

reports I prepared. Can you bind enough copies for the meeting? If you're stuck I'll come and help you.' Caz touched a hand to her forehead, aware that she sounded desperate. It only made her feel worse when her PA was at pains to reassure her. Julie would have guessed that all the executives at Brent would be tense this morning. But she was more wound up than most, and coffee wasn't the answer. And now she must forget everything but work.

'Oh, that's easy,' Caz informed the empty room. Her body was screaming with sexual frustration, while she was in the throes of some deeper, inner grief. Her concentration levels were at zero.

It was just after nine when Julie came back on the intercom. 'I know you said no calls, but I thought this is one you should respond to…'

Reluctant to lift her head from her work, Caz hummed agreement.

'Mr Brent wants to see you in his office now.'

'Now?' Caz's throat dried. Business was an arena in which she excelled, but today it was as if the essence of success were being fed through the air-conditioning system making even Cassandra doubt her abilities. Brent the Younger came with a formidable reputation, which had put everyone on edge. Everyone except Cassandra Bailey Brown, Caz reassured herself, patting her hair and then standing to smooth her slim black pencil skirt.

'Don't worry,' Julie chirruped, 'you'll knock him dead.'

* * *

Counting to ten wasn't enough, so she counted to ten again and then knocked on the mahogany door, which already bore the legend: Chairman.

Brent the Younger had chosen a smaller office than the one previously occupied by his father, his reason being that as he would move between the various plants he didn't need to monopolise such a large space. As long as he had a window and a view he was content, apparently. And his view stretched way down the newly restored canal. It was one of the few open aspects in the building and everyone envied him. They had also notched up the fact that, as well as modest, he was shrewd.

And so was she, Caz reassured herself. She just had to convince herself that she was firing on all cylinders, ready for anything…

'Hello, Caz.'

'Galem…' Caz stood transfixed in the doorway, and then it was as if a veil had been lifted and she couldn't believe she had been so dense. Drawing herself up, she walked forward with her head held high, her future, her life, her sheer existence hanging like a delicate silken thread between them. 'I'm sorry, I mean Mr Brent…' As Galem rose from his seat behind the desk Caz extended her hand ready for the traditional greeting.

He ignored her outstretched hand and sat down again, indicating a chair. 'Everyone calls me Galem and that includes you, Caz.'

Caz remained standing. There was no warmth in

Galem's voice, and his eyes were cold. She felt sick inside, but at the same time a catalogue of charges against him were forming in her mind. He had betrayed her trust, deceiving her in the most unforgivable way. He had misled her from the start, taken her virginity, slept with her, not once, but many times, knowing he was her boss. He had lied to her.

But she was blameless?

Caz lashed herself a few times with the word hypocrite before taking her seat, and as she did so she thought about the weekend and her anger changed to a deep-rooted sadness. Both were feelings she had no option but to stifle. Above all she wanted to hold onto her job with Brent. She had a deep emotional attachment to the company that had given her the first leg up in life, and on a practical level there would be no Stone Break House, no penthouse in Leeds, no food on the table, no car, no clothes, no Caz Ryan. And right now Galem Brent held all that in the palm of his hand.

As well as holding her life in his hands Galem was holding her personnel file, Caz noticed, flicking through it with his long, tanned fingers. She cleared her throat in an attempt to bury the thought of other places those fingers had explored, but those places were already tingling. His mouth…his lips… Caz eased her neck, trying to forget, but then Galem lifted his head from the file, catapulting her back to the present with a look that held none of the warmth she remembered from those previous encounters.

He put the file down on the desk in front of him,

lining it up next to a file she didn't recognise. She knew that everything she had worked for was about to slip away and there was nothing she could do about it but sit and wait. The thought of what was at stake launched her on an agonising journey that took her from a children's home to a ditch in Hawkshead, and on again through each preconception and glaring error of judgement she had formed about Galem Brent. The fact that she had been made a director of his company specifically because of her talent for reading people didn't escape her reckoning.

Picking up one of the files, Galem studied it. Dressed in ripped jeans and a frayed Aran sweater he had been stunning, but here in the office with his thick black hair neatly groomed and wearing a dark business suit, garnished with a silk tie and crisp white shirt, he made her heart thunder. Or maybe that was apprehension stalking her…

'I'm going to call for coffee,' he said. Leaning over the desk, he buzzed his PA and placed his order.

They were going to be there for some time, Caz deduced, sitting tensely on the edge of the chair.

'So. Caz,' Galem said, sitting back. 'Or should I say Cassandra?'

His expression told her he knew everything, and her heart clenched at the thought of what that meant. Her head was reeling and she was having trouble finding business mode, but she forced herself to examine the facts. She wouldn't be sitting here if she had fallen short in her job, but had she hung herself with the rope Galem had given her during the weekend? There'd been enough of it, after all. She was sure the answer lay somewhere inside the folders he had in front of him.

'Do you know what these are?'

'My personnel folder, and… I'm afraid I don't recognise the other one.'

He picked it up, and then there was a brief pause as his PA came in with a tray of coffee.

His eyes were tourmaline, Caz thought as her mind felt free to wander briefly, and were the same colour as the silk thread in his tie. His suit had undoubtedly been tailor-made for him, by some famous designer, she guessed, judging by the vivid lining. How could she have made such a peerlessly bad judgement call?

Galem glanced her way as his PA poured coffee for them both. His face appeared impassive, but she sensed beneath it was the confidence of a predator, who knowing all the strengths and weaknesses of his prey, could afford to toy with it for a bit.

When the woman left the room and shut the door he said, 'Your appointment as a director of my company is a significant achievement, Caz.'

'Thank you.'

'You hold down a position of great trust here at Brent.'

Warning bells rang inside her and everything started to tighten.

'You're privy to a lot of confidential financial in-formation, for example.'

She could only nod agreement. She had discov-ered that directors at Brent, highly trusted individu-als all of them, were given the access codes to just about everything on the system.

'Therefore,' Galem went on, straightening up again, 'it won't surprise you to learn that there are companies who specialise in carrying out security checks for me.'

Now there was only a body in a chair, and that body was Caz Ryan. Cassandra Bailey Brown was floating somewhere overhead waving goodbye to Caz and her precious career.

'Naturally, the company I employ carried out a full check on you.'

Some people could get angry in order to intimidate, while others could be equally threatening with just the use of a low voice and a direct stare. Galem was one of them. When she had compiled her CV invention had seemed her only option. She still didn't know what she could have done differently to get a job, to get a break, and wasn't going to sit mute now and not defend herself. 'I'd do it again,' she said. 'Perhaps you had the luxury of a home, a family, and a direction in life. I had none of those things. I had to live on my wits. And before you accuse me of feeling sorry for myself, let me put you right. I have never felt sorry for myself. In fact I think I've been lucky because I've always been free to take whatever path I chose in life—'

'And you chose Brent. Why?'

Galem shot the question at her while she was still recovering from his opening salvo. He was as merciless as Cassandra, but why did she expect anything less of him? Caz firmed her jaw. 'I didn't choose Brent, Brent chose me. Your father took a chance on me, spent money on my training; gave me day release to attend university—'

'So your loyalty is unquestioned?'

'Absolutely.' She held his stare.

'Your track record with Brent shows you're a highly motivated individual, as well as being a loyal member of the team.'

A loyal member of the team? Brent had given her purpose, and had become both her home and her family. She had already lost Galem; was she going to lose that too?

'This is the report I received,' he said, pushing a folder across the desk. 'You might want to look it over.'

She didn't need to look at it; she knew what it would say.

'You got a good degree,' he said, launching straight in, 'but there's no mention of a secondary school in your file…'

'Yes, there is,' she said confidently, before she could stop herself. She was so used to living in the past she had invented she couldn't stop even though this was the man who could end her career with the stroke of his pen.

'Ah, yes,' Galem said, tilting the file round as if he hadn't memorised every word, 'Princess Amelia's school for girls in Switzerland, wasn't it?' His brows rose as he looked at her. 'Swanky. You just made one elementary mistake.' He paused to ramp up her discomfort. 'Princess Amelia's school isn't a secondary school, it's what they call a finishing school. Young ladies attend post A levels in order to learn how to win a wealthy husband.' He looked at her. 'That doesn't sound like you, Caz. There was no finishing school for Caz Ryan, was there? You grew up in a children's home.'

She held his gaze, refusing to flinch, refusing to show any emotion at all under Galem's remorseless stare. What was the point in denying it, when everything he said was true?

CHAPTER SIXTEEN

'LET'S forget Cassandra and concentrate on Caz Ryan,' Galem said, settling back in his chair.

'Back-street girl from the children's home?'

'Caz Ryan from the children's home,' Galem said, ignoring the interruption. 'The same Caz Ryan who was helped, financially, through university and then managed to achieve a reasonable degree while holding down three jobs. None of which, by the way, had the slightest relevance to my business.'

She wanted to leap across the desk and shake him. Only remembering what was at stake held her back. She had constructed the type of CV she had known would get her the job with Brent. She'd been young, desperate and equally determined, and she'd had too many disappointments in the past to risk telling the truth.

'You lied to me—'

Galem was judging her? 'And you lied to me.'

But his deception had been a very personal one,

and raising what had happened between them in Hawkshead in these sterile business surroundings expanded her accusation into something stark and shocking. She went for broke. 'From the moment you found out who I was the only thing on your mind was Stone Break House, and you were prepared to stop at nothing to get it. You used me, Galem.'

Caz's words reverberated in the silence.

'Are you saying that I forced you to do anything you didn't want to do?'

'Of course not.' Blood rushed to her cheeks. They might have been discussing business for all the emotion in Galem's voice, while her head was full of Galem kissing her, Galem holding her, Galem re-assuring her… Didn't he feel anything, anything at all?

Caz's stomach roiled and her heart was beating so fast she could hardly breathe. It was all she could do to maintain the mask of composure she'd stuck on her face at the outset of the meeting. 'My point, Galem, is that I didn't know who you were, and you didn't see any reason to tell me, but you knew who I was all along.'

'And wasn't it more convenient for you to lose the virginity that had become such an embarrassment to you to a rough paver from Hawkshead than anyone else? Wasn't anonymity your safeguard? Hasn't it always been the shield you hide behind, Caz?'

She could make no excuses, but hurt was piling

high on top of her humiliation, and she wasn't going down without a fight. 'You have a reputation for being ruthless in business and you brought those same tactics into our lives regardless of how that would make me feel when I discovered the truth. You're every bit as much a fraud as I am, Galem.'

'I never pretended to be anything other than the person I am. It was you who assumed and drew conclusions. And whatever I did or didn't do over the weekend, it doesn't affect the business.'

Cassandra would have known that. Cassandra would have been as incisive as Galem; she wouldn't have allowed herself to be distracted by personal considerations as Caz had.

'Did you really think Cassandra would change your life?'

She refocused as Galem barked the question at her.

'You must have done; to the extent that you changed your name by deed poll.' His lips tugged down with distaste. 'I can't think of anyone who would willingly sign up to a lifetime membership of the blinkered, prejudiced, self-serving minority like you did, and I have to ask myself, is this the type of person I want on my board?'

'A name doesn't change me, Galem.'

He let the silence hang. 'Is there anything else you'd like to say to me?' he said at last.

'No, I don't think so.' What could she say?

It seemed impossible that there would be a way

back from this. Silence was buzzing between them like an angry insect, and Caz found herself retreating inwardly from all the angry voices in her head. She took refuge in a void of sadness. She knew there was another man beneath Galem's driven shell, and that man was warm and humorous and kind, so Galem Brent wasn't so different from Caz Ryan, after all.

'I can offer you my resignation if you want it,' she said, 'but there's a meeting soon, and I have an obligation to the team. And I won't make apologies for who I am and what I did. I'm proud of what I've achieved, Galem, and neither you nor anyone else can take that away from me.' She was twisting her hands in her lap, Caz realised, stilling them. She had no intention of breaking down in front of Galem. But emotion was building up in her and something had to give. She got up clumsily, almost knocking the chair over in her haste to leave the room.

Galem came after her, moving in front of her as she reached the lift. 'Have you eaten anything?'

His hand was up by her face, resting on the doors of the lift. She stared at him blankly, her mind in uproar. Her thoughts were a crazy mix of the sight and scent of Galem, together with grief at what they'd lost, and all of it packaged in the determination not to let her colleagues down before she left the building.

'Have you had breakfast?' he said again.

Food was the last thing on her mind. After staying

the night at Stone Break House she'd called the taxi service to bring her into Leeds. She'd been too anxious for food at the apartment, knowing this was a big day for her, the day when she finally got to meet the chairman of Brent Construction. She'd changed her mind about which suit to wear at least three times and then had polished Cassandra's leather briefcase before scuffing it again in case it looked unused, and all that before closing the door on her apartment. And then arriving at the office, instead of concentrating on work as she had intended her head had been full of Galem; her heart too. Breakfast? No. She hadn't eaten a thing since the previous day.

'I thought not,' Galem said, standing aside so she could go past him when the lift doors opened. 'I'll have something sent down to your office.'

'Thank you,' Caz said formally, stepping inside the lift, but when their eyes met her stomach jounced, and her eyes threatened to fill with tears again. She was in love with him. Whatever the future held, she loved him, this man who held her career in the palm of his hand. She had felt comfortable and relaxed with her sexy paver, and for the first time in her life she'd had the courage to be herself. But this wasn't her affable, sexy paver this was Galem Brent, the chairman of Brent Construction, a man who had taken his father's business and turned it into a world-class corporation. And he hadn't done that by being soft.

'Or on second thoughts… Perhaps I should come with you and make sure you don't fall into anything, or over anything, or stamp on anyone's feet.'

The air left her lungs in a rush as Galem stepped into the lift just as the doors were closing, but his face remained impassive, so she had no way of knowing what was going through his mind.

She'd already keyed in her floor but he hit the button for the basement car park. 'The view's spectacular, isn't it?' he said, refusing to explain this as the panoramic lift swooped down the side of the building.

She was still stunned, still wondering why he was in the lift with her, added to which she hated lifts, hated heights, hated being in this impossible position. 'The view? How can you act as though we've never met?' Caz was instantly furious with herself. She'd been so determined to say nothing, to keep her cool and preserve what tiny shreds of her pride remained, and now, not only had she thrown all that away she had done it with the crassest of theatrical flourishes.

Galem's expression didn't change, but he touched something on the control panel and the lift stopped mid-floor. 'I'm sorry,' he said coolly. 'Did you expect me to send round a company e-mail announcing the fact that we'd spent the weekend in bed?'

'I'll give you my resignation' Fumbling furiously in her briefcase, she dragged out a pen and some paper. 'Here,' she said. 'I can write it for you now.'

'I don't want it,' Galem said, brushing her hand away. 'You're too good for Brent for me to lose you.'

But not good enough for you. Caz shook her head. 'I won't stay. How can I? How do you expect me to work alongside you now?'

'That's up to you, Caz,' Galem said, touching the control panel again.

So that was it, Caz thought, squeezing her eyes shut. She was back to square one. She only cared about work, and that was the coin by which she was valued. Cassandra won, after all.

But as the lift started down the woman inside her told Cassandra to beat it. 'You left Hawkshead without even saying goodbye to me, Galem—'

'So did you.'

'I tried to see you before I left.'

'Was that before you put the keys to the cottage through the letterbox, got in a taxi and drove away?'

She stared at him. 'I spent the night at Stone Break House.'

'And I left you to say goodbye to your friends and then I went to check the dogs and say goodbye to Thomas. When I got back to the cottage, you'd packed up and gone.'

And the last place you would have looked for me at night was Stone Break House, Caz thought as Galem stood to one side to let her pass when the lift doors slid open.

'What are you doing? Where are you taking me?' He was steering her towards the car park.

'On a journey.'

'No, I can't. I've got work to do—'

'And I'm giving you the rest of the day off.' To close off her only escape route, he placed a call, postponing the meeting to the next day.

'Get in the car, Caz.' Galem opened the passenger door of a black Range Rover Vogue. 'This is something we both need to do.'

'Why?' She hesitated. 'I can't see the point. I can't see where this is going—'

'Get in.'

It took Cassandra to remind her that her job hung in the balance.

They drove in silence through the city and took the link road onto the motorway. Galem was a good driver, smooth and controlled, and the vehicle he drove was the epitome of luxury. Caz knew he was taking her back to Hawkshead, but she was curious to know why. When they approached Stone Break House she asked him. 'I got the impression you didn't want me here in Hawkshead. What's changed, Galem?'

'I don't seem to have made a very good job of getting rid of you, do I?' The glance he shot her made her heart race.

'So what is it about Stone Break House?' she asked as he drew up outside.

If he told her she would think it another ploy to soften her up and buy the house through the back door, but he hadn't made the journey to say nothing.

'Stone Break House was my childhood home where I grew up. I came back here to retrace my roots, to understand what made my father tick, and, of course, to buy it back from the new owner.'

'So the weekend with me was all part of your plan?'

'I didn't plan for you to drive your car into a ditch.'

'But once you realised who I was you realised you had a golden opportunity.' Caz was warming to her theory when Galem stopped her.

'Nothing half so complicated,' he said, leaning forward to stare her in the eyes. 'I wanted to take you to bed.'

His frankness shocked her; made her angry too. 'How long have you known you were my boss?'

'From the moment you told me your name. I felt sure there couldn't be two Cassandra Bailey Browns in the world.'

'So, where do I stand?' Caz said as he switched off the engine.'

'This isn't about work, Caz. There are more things in life, in case you hadn't noticed?'

She had. 'So why are we here?' She stared out of the window at the house.

'Because I think Aunt Maud intended this all along,' Galem said, removing the keys in readiness to get out. 'Maybe she blamed herself for not being close to your mother—for not being in a position to rescue you from that children's home. I can't be sure of anything; I only know she grew fond of me when I used to visit.'

'That's a pretty wild supposition.'

'Can you come up with a better idea?'

'Coincidence.'

'That's just as unreliable.'

'I can see why Aunt Maud might leave the house to me, but why would she want to bring us together?'

'My connection with your aunt goes back to the days when my mother had an affair with a rival contractor. She left Stone Break House one Christmas Eve, wrapping a scarf around my neck and hustling me down the road in the dark. My father never recovered from that, though eventually he was consoled by his secretary.'

'Aunt Maud?' Caz said quietly. 'And knowing all this you slept with me?'

'I made love to you.'

She looked at him, wanting so desperately to believe that was true.

'I fell in love with you,' Galem said, with a self-deprecating shrug. 'No one was more surprised than me. Love at first sight; that's what they call it, isn't it?'

'Or love in a ditch, maybe…' She smiled a little, wanting to believe him so badly.

'I suspected you felt the same—'

'I did.'

'I have my own insecurities. I had to be sure you were falling in love with me, and not with Galem

Brent, the chairman of Brent Construction. Cassandra might have seen that as a career move. But as I got to know you better I wanted more than that, I wanted to challenge *all* your perceptions.'

'And you wanted Stone Break House?'

'Yes, but I'm greedy; I want it all.'

'You really mean that, don't you?'

'Let's do this together, Caz…you and me.'

'What are you saying, Galem?'

Leaning across, he placed a finger beneath her chin and tipped her face up so he could stare into her eyes. 'Let's bury Cassandra in the foundations of the tennis court where we can jump on her every day. Let's get married and share the back-breaking work that lies ahead of us if we're going to stop this old house falling down. And…' reaching inside her briefcase, he plucked out her scribbled letter of resignation '…let's never talk again about unsettling the delicate balance I have established on the board of Brent Construction.'

'Dinosaur,' Caz accused him softly as Galem ripped her letter to shreds in front of her eyes. 'Do you think you're going to get everything your own way, from now on?' Her heart was leaping around insanely as he stared into her eyes.

'I think we've both got a very challenging future in front of us, and I for one wouldn't have it any other way. Will you marry me, Caz Ryan?'

Her mouth moved but no sound came out. Caz glanced at the house and then at Galem.

'I love you a lot more than bricks and mortar.'

'And what if I won't marry you?'

'We'll just have to live in sin.' His lips tugged up, sending heat flooding through her. 'But one thing's for sure, that house won't come to life until we're both living there under the same roof.'

'The same leaky roof.'

'Is that a yes, Caz? Only I'm an impatient man.'

'How impatient? It's just that maybe I need a little more persuading,' she teased.

Galem reached across and pulled her onto his lap. 'That's fine with me.' It was a tight fit in the Range Rover, and hugely difficult wearing constricting business clothes, but somehow they made it with Caz telling herself that it had to be a lot more comfortable than the beat-up tractor. The luxurious leather seats were comfortable and firm, and the broad span of windscreen was a great place to rest her feet. The windows were soon steamed up, and it was quite a while before they were ready to start their tour of the house.

They were just walking through the gates arm in arm when Galem's phone went off. From the set of his shoulders Caz knew immediately that something was wrong. 'Is it bad news?'

'Sally's gone missing…'

Their world was like a see-saw that went up and down. Sheer happiness was instantly replaced with sheer horror at the thought that the adoring greyhound with her big mournful eyes could have been hurt or worse. All Caz could think was how lucky it was that they had arrived in Hawkshead just at the right time. She turned straight back to the Range Rover, but not before she noticed Galem's glance sweep over her smart black business suit. 'Forget it,' she told him. 'We have to go right now and look for her. Is it possible she ran away?'

'That's one possibility, but with Sid as their father her pups will be valuable.'

'You don't think she's been stolen, do you? Oh, Galem, come on…' She grabbed his arm. 'There's no time to lose.'

He smiled as she did her tottering little run in her too-tight skirt and five-inch heels; there were some parts of Caz Ryan he hoped would never change.

They eventually found Sally in the grounds of Stone Break House. The contented mother was curled up in a ball beneath some bushes, and for a moment as Galem cradled the greyhound's head in his arms Caz thought she might be hurt. Her mouth dried as she asked the question. 'Is she all right?'

'All right?'

Caz's heart lurched as Galem turned to smile at her. 'Come and see for yourself.'

There were six tiny, blind, pink hairless puppies scrabbling for position around their mother's milk-swollen belly. Caz knelt in the mud at Galem's side, exclaiming with pleasure. 'They're so beautiful… Do you think there's a champion in the litter?' she said, turning her face up to Galem.

'Maybe, but they're all beautiful to me. Will you help me get them in the car?'

They made a bed of leaves in the boot and Galem very gently laid the greyhound Sally down on top of it. Caz followed him with the puppies in her arms, carrying them three at a time until mother and babies were reunited and made comfortable.

They took the new family back to Old Thomas, who had remained at the kennels to be there in case Sally wandered home. The rest of the village was out searching for her and Thomas promised to ring round and make sure everyone heard the good news. Sid was ecstatic and couldn't stop licking his beloved mate's face. Caz was sure the handsome greyhound stood a little taller once he had surveyed his litter of new pups.

'Thank you for coming to search for Sally,' Galem said as they strolled back to the car.

'I'm just so relieved I can't tell you…'

Galem could stare into her eyes like no one else on earth, and at one time she would have been frightened by how much he could see, but now she couldn't hide how much she loved him. He could still make her blush with that look. 'I must look a mess,' she said, staring down at her ripped tights and ruined skirt.

'I think you look very sexy.'

'You do?'

He nodded but then laughed. 'Okay, I promise to buy you some rugged outdoor clothing,' he said, draping an arm over her shoulder, 'if only to hide those parts of you I find so distracting.'

Air shot from her lungs as Galem nuzzled her neck. 'That would be a shame.'

Then they both looked at each other and laughed as Sid and Sally started barking.

'They're encouraging us,' Galem insisted.

'Will they be all right now?'

'Of course they will.'

'Why do you think Sally ran away?'

'Even dogs need space sometimes.'

'Is that a hint?' Caz slanted a stare at Galem, daring him to agree.

'No, that wasn't a hint.' Stopping, he turned to face her, and, taking her face between his hands, he drew her close. 'We work well as a team, Caz.'

'Do we?'

'You know it. I'm on board for Stone Break House, aren't I?'

'But am I on your board?' Her anxiety was showing, Caz realised.

'You're part of everything I do,' Galem said, turning suddenly serious. Then grinning his bad-boy smile again, he brushed her mouth with his lips, teasing her and nipping her in a way that could only lead to one thing.

'Do you have nothing better to do than make love all day?' She pretended to complain, but this time it was Galem's turn to think of practicalities.

'I'd better feed you first, hadn't I? Don't want to wear you out before the wedding. And I know just the place…'

'Steak and chips?' Galem said, picking up the menu at the pub. 'Or would you prefer something lighter?'

'Like pie and peas?'

They shared a look, which made Caz feel all warm and fuzzy inside. In just three days they were sharing a history. She liked that, it felt good. But she couldn't help thinking that there was too big a gulf between Galem Brent, boss of Brent Construction, and Caz Ryan from the children's home.

'Penny for them,' Galem said, leading her to a table with a little bit of privacy. 'All right for you here?' He held her chair.

'Fine.' She sat down.

'So, what's on your mind, Caz?'

'Nothing…'

'You can't lie to me, not any more.' Leaning across the small round wooden table, Galem caught hold of her fidgety hands and enclosed them in his giant fist.

'I never could lie to you…'

He smiled at her. 'So, what is it? What's worrying you?'

'We come from different worlds—'

'Not that old chestnut.' Galem threw himself back in his seat, lips pressing down in mock disapproval. 'You were Caz, and then you were Cassandra and now you're Caz again. But here's the thing—both Cassandra and Caz live in the same world I do. And that's an end of it, as far as I'm concerned.' Leaning across the table, he held her gaze. 'Cassandra Ryan, will you marry me?'

'You know I will.'

'Well, there's your answer. Now, what do you want to eat? For goodness' sake, hurry up and make your mind up. I'm starving.'

'Pie, peas *and* chips?'

'Your wish is my command, lovely lady,' Galem said, dipping to plant a tender kiss on Caz's neck as he left the table to place their order.

EPILOGUE

THERE was always a handkerchief of blue sky over Hawkshead. That was what Galem had told her, and he was right, except that it had rained all night and the ground over which she had hoped to sweep her Vera Wang wedding dress was thick with mud.

That was no problem for Caz, except that the vintage Rolls Cassandra had pictured herself arriving in at the small village chapel got stuck in the approach to Stone Break House.

Caz quickly found a solution: wellington boots and a lift on Galem's ancient tractor. Now, admittedly the tractor was garlanded with white roses picked from the garden and the buckles on her Hunter boots were threaded through with white ribbons, but she cut quite a picture all the same. In flowing tulle, with a sweep train tucked into her boots, and a beautiful lace overlay on a low-cut sweetheart bodice topped off with a sensible waterproof jacket, just in case. She had to laugh at her image of country chic.

Well, this was Yorkshire, not Mauritius where Galem was taking her to spend their honeymoon in a wooden hut suspended over the ocean in a sumptuous five-star resort.

Caz didn't know what to expect when Old Thomas drew the tractor to a halt outside the chapel doors. Would she find Galem, her sexy paver, waiting, or Galem, the chairman of Brent Construction?

The one—or, rather, two things she could be sure about was that Stone Break Sid and Hawkshead Sally were waiting for her at their door, their leashes in the safe keeping of the plump lady from the village hall. Each greyhound had a tasteful silk ribbon in shades of peach, ivory and aqua round their necks, as, naturally, the tasteful colour scheme for the wedding had been chosen by Cassandra.

The low throb of country music greeted her as she walked through the door on the arm of Old Thomas who had cleaned up really well for the occasion, and was wearing his best Elvis suit, complete with diamante studs. Hugo and Cordelia sat down quietly at the back after politely showing everyone to their places. Galem had decreed that their business acumen far outweighed their snobbishness, and with the mettle of true survivors both of them had adapted quickly to his ways.

This was a fairy story, Caz thought as she walked up the aisle towards her prince. And there just weren't enough of them these days—not for grown-ups, anyway.

I love you, Galem mouthed as she approached, and she was thrilled to see the tears brightening his ocean-green eyes.

'I'm so proud of you,' he murmured.

'Me, too,' Caz replied as Sally the greyhound panted her approval. Each dog had been given special dispensation to enter the church and Sally had been given the special honour of bearing the rings.

Galem's was a simple platinum band—suitable either for a paver or for the chairman of an international corporation—while Caz's was a little more exotic. Cassandra and Caz had come to an accommodation in the months following Galem's proposal. Cassandra was pleased to accept Galem's solitaire diamond ring from Tiffany's, and, if Caz almost fainted with shock when she saw the size of it, Cassandra had helped her to maintain her cool and poise so that in the end she didn't disgrace herself. Her wedding band was a similar fabulosity. A band of diamonds flashed like fire on the ruby velvet cushion suspended on a golden chain beneath Sally the greyhound's head.

'If you've got it, why not flaunt it?' had been Galem's flimsy excuse for the extravagance. And who was Caz to argue when she had Cassandra prompting her from the wings?

'Oh, okay, then,' she had managed graciously, trying not to pass out from pleasure as Galem had tried it on her for size.

And now old Thomas was placing her hand in Galem's. She looked up at him. Galem was the same man, with the same rugged face and the same thick black hair that she had first fallen in love with. His ocean-green eyes were the same, his sensual lips just as kissable, and the broad spread of his shoulders beneath the formal tail suit still rang her bell.

'I hope I haven't disgraced you?' he said.

'How could you?' Caz murmured, thinking him the most handsome man she had ever seen—not to mention the most well dressed.

Until Galem discreetly glanced towards the ground and she saw his feet.

Cassandra gasped. Caz laughed. Those kick-the-door-down boots looked just great to her.

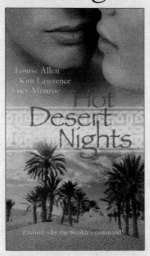

0607/25/MB093

*What lurks beneath the surface
of the powerful and prestigious
Chrighton Dynasty?*

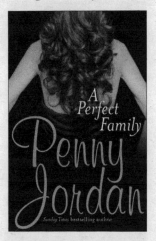

As three generations of the Chrighton family
gather for a special birthday celebration, no one
could possibly have anticipated that their secure
world was about to be rocked by the events of
one fateful weekend.

One dramatic revelation leads to another
– a secret war-time liaison, a carefully concealed
embezzlement scam, the illicit seduction of
somebody else's wife.

And the results are going to be explosive…

Available 1st June 2007

www.millsandboon.co.uk